DEDICATION:

I simply dedicate this book to God and God alone.
Thank you father God, you always deserve my best.

DON'T MISS BOOK#1 IN 'BEAUTIFULLY UGLY PEOPLE' SERIES

I AM WHAT I DO

Have you ever woke up one morning and felt like you didn't belong? You looked in the mirror at your life and said, 'Why did God make me who I am, why can't I just be someone different?' Why do I have to feel so bad about myself when my wrong doings feels so good? I mean, I do wrong because I can, not necessarily because I want to. Many times when I do wrong, it seems like I have no control over my actions. At the time I'm in the moment, I just blank out and wave the white flag. Everyday I live for something; waiting for something different in school to happen, wishing my parents Rodney and Sandra Lewis were back together again.

As I twist and turn through the hallways, I realize that when my parents broke up, I not only lost my father, but I also lost my soul. Now, here I am sitting in the front of my mother's class, as she teaches creative writing classes. To be truly honest with myself, I hate creative writing. I really find nothing creative in it. If you ask me, creative writing is for the birds, because all I see is authors trying to use big words, move your imagination a little

7

and get paid for that crap.

As a matter of fact, people actually pay to read books written by some person somewhere out in the country who has no life (what so ever). Me, I love to chill, smoke, and kick back with my home-boys. I love my mom. She's the only motivation I have for being in this class. My sister Precious and I have come a long way since the divorce. I have teachers complaining to my mom everyday, saying what I did or did not do. I know she hates that mess.

My art teacher gets on our nerves. Some-times I am ready to punch that brother in the mouth. That art teacher always addresses me like I am a kid. Well, I'm not little Justin any more. I became the man in the house when Pops decided to run off with Ms. Hamburger.

Personally, I'm just fed up. I'm tired of being looked at as the one whom suppose to change the hearts and minds of thousands of kids. I mean, what do they expect from me? I'm only sixteen! I like to hang out and I definitely don't see myself as a suspenders wearing role model. Yet all the teachers love to hoop and holler about my Mom being such a great example to her students, therefore I need to be that example as well. Bull crap!

To any of ya'll teachers who have the self-re-spect not to kiss up to my mom to get to me, here's what I've got to say. I am an example of an American dream wasted, the poster child for drugs, sex and countless women. So if you want to know who I got it from; then ask my daddy and ask his daddy, he'll tell you about it. It's called a generational curse. For all of you whom don't believe in it, ask your grandmother about it; or your pimping uncle or your slanderous aunt, you'll really start to see how much of them is really in you.

I'm Not proud to be apart of a generational curse, and if you ask me, the whole thing sounds pretty scary to begin with. I truly wish that I can break that sucka, but right now I got to deal with it. I'm not trying to say that the generational curse is any excuse to live out my perverted fantasies and stuff. But, I am saying that it's got something to do with this American dream gone bad.

Last night I was watching the television, and as I was surfing channels, I saw this pastor dude talking to the audience, telling them they need to get their life right with Christ. I mean I thought that the pastor was wrong for saying what he said because from my understanding, any one who commits his or herself to a church commits themselves to Christ. I ain't been in the church for a good six years, since I was like ten, but I know that I'm a Christian because of the time I did go. These pastors have a lot to learn, accusing those people of not being right with Christ. What's up with that?

I know this Spanish chick who loves to talk about Jesus. I love Jesus, but apparently not as much as she does. Every time I slip up just a tiny wee bit, she's always trying to over correct me, and make me feel like I'm going to hell. Just because of a small little sin, not to mention she's got some skeletons in her closet too, if you know what I mean.

I love to call her Saint Maria for all the scriptures she loves to go toe to toe with me on. If you ask me I truly think the girl got the gift of gab, and she knows how to twist and turn the Bible to fit her lifestyle accordingly.

In Maria's eyes, she is one of God's little angels sent down from heaven to take back the church. Which brings me to another theory: why would God want to be taking back a church that's already His? I mean it makes no sense at all to me. But there's no need to debate Saint Maria because usually she claims to know it all, and I being the Lost Christian know absolutely nothing.

I'm only sixteen years old. Why do I need to be a Fully Found Christian at this age in my life? I've got my whole life ahead of me: who can stand against that? Well, nobody but God. Nobody but God. My father used to tell my sister and me stories about God all the time. When we were little, I was so impressed. I believed my father and every one of those stories till I found out he cheated on mama.

I loved the story about David against Goliath and Daniel in the lions' den. But now, as I think about those stories, they tend to make very little sense to me. I watch pro-football and I have yet to see a three hundred and sixty five pound lineman get run over by this little one-hundred and fifty pound running back.

If I saw some phenomenon like that happening, I'd be doing some personal recruiting myself.

And as for Daniel being in the lions den, I really can't say whether that makes sense or not because it all boils down to whether the lions' were hungry. That would be the number one question. The number two question would be: since when were humans apart of the lion food chain? And if we are, Lord have mercy on us!

School is for jerks and time is never on my side, it's almost like a train that never finds its destination. School passes by my eyes over and over as I watch the teachers' horrified. When I was a kid I used to love school, even though I had this one teacher that gave me stacks of work. Now, all I want to do is get out, get loose and get gone from here.

From time to time my pops comes by on surprise visits, as if he really gives a crap about my education. In all honesty, I don't give a crap about my education, but to make matters worse I'm passing all my classes. I think that my pops just come around here to spy on moms, but that's just what I think. Otherwise I believe the playa' might as well play around somewhere else. I mean, doesn't he get it? He needs to move on to someone else because Moms got her a man. Enough about him. There I was believing in him and he messed around and cheated on Moms. Life ain't never been the same since.

Moms got her a boyfriend she's been dating for the past two years. So she's definitely moving forward with her life. Moving forward, what a phrase, wonder why far too many people find it hard to do? Never the less, I can understand the fear, the emotions, and anxiety that a playa' gets when he or she gets hurt in a relationship. I mean, Moms took years to finally get over Dad, and at times she still cries over the loser. It makes me sick, just thinking about the way he left us, for Ms. Hamburger.

I must say, the last time I saw Ms. Hamburger; she was looking fine as a dime. As far as lust is concerned, yeah, I can see why he dabbled with Ms. Hamburger. But that still doesn't give him an excuse to have sex with her, profound Deacon in the church or not.

Enough about my stupid family issues. As anyone can tell I'm still not over the hurt that my dad put us through. So I guess I'm really the one that's not ready to move on. Ten years ago my father did the unthinkable, and ten years later I'm still holding it against him.

These last couple of years, I've been dealing with the sleepless nights, and time and time again coming to Moms' rescue and handing her a piece of tissue at one o'clock in the morning. Sometimes Precious even woke up, as Mom just wailed herself to sleep. The torment and hurt I've seen on her face was the kind of look that was etched in my memory. As a matter of fact, it seems as if my Mom's been a lot happier these past two years than any time she ever spent with Dad. I can tell that she still gets anxious and nervous when he comes around for even a minute.

That Bastard, I hate him, yet, I love him because he's my father. I am his seed. But wow, God!

Why did this have to happen to *my* family? I never *asked* to be born, and I'm *sure* mom didn't ask to be cheated on. O loving God that they say you are, do you hear me?

Man, please! God ain't listening. If he was, things would have went a lot smoother. He would have warned Mom about the pornography, and Ms. Hamburger. But who am I? I'm just a little ant crawling this earth, asking for attention from The Man in the sky, who created me in His image. The funniest thing about being created in His image: I never get to see him! So there you have it, God. I'm upset with you too! You've seen all the signs, all the habits he picked up, but You did nothing about it!

The other day I heard one of my hard core Christian classmates say, "Only God can judge me." Tell me this, God! Who's there to judge You? When you cause fire to come down from heaven and burn up thousands of men. When you create a hurricane or earthquake and say that you do it because You love us. God that doesn't sound like love. That sounds like a crazy woman going through P.M.S. Please, don't strike me down!

Enough about that, I'm about to blow this joint in a minute. Yes. Only ten minutes till the bell rings. Home free, people, home free.

Here comes Principal Adams. "Mr. Lewis, will you please follow me to my office? I have a few things to discuss with you. You know, maybe a word of advice that your mother refuses to give you," the principal turned on her spiked heels expecting me

13

to follow.

What does this mean old Principal Lady want from me now? Heard this lady has been around since the dinosaurs. Her and my Moms' don't get along. So I think Dr. Adams tries to take it out on me. The lady needs to get a life quick, or I'm running to a higher authority to get her butt fired or something. Shoot, nobody likes her at school; she's like a dog that needs to be put on a leash or else she'll be all over the place crapping on teachers, telling them what they ain't doing right.

Yep, that's what Dr. Adams does; she craps on teachers and barks at students. The lady needs to retire. Sho'nuff.

"I'll be right there in a minute, Ms. Adams," I said respectfully, yet raging inside.

"It's *Dr.* Adams to you son, and I'm tired of correcting you and your Mother on that. Actually, you know son, you can call me *Mrs.* Adams because I am happily married for four years. You got that Justin?" *Who would marry her?*

"Yes ma'am." I ground my teeth because that lady just makes a person want to pimp slap her in the face. *Happily married huh? Yeah right! She seems like a miserable hag on steroids. I wonder what it is she's trying to talk to me about anyways. I've got after school activities and the band is one of them.*

"Come on in, have a seat Justin. Let's chat shall we? First of all, let me give it to you straight: Your conduct, in my opinion, sucks! If it wasn't for your union crazed Mother, you'd already be expelled from my school, son. Got that?" She lectured me.

"Wait a minute, Mrs. Adams. You don't have to bring my Moms into this. This is between me and you," I got her straight quick.

"It's you and me. I guess that English class is not working for you?" she sneered. *I swear I'm about to swing on this lady if she says another word.* "Right, so you're the adult now Justin and I need permission to talk to you about your Mom? Ok, fair enough, adult.

You screw up one more time in those classes: Giving your art teacher a hard time and throwing paper across your math class? I'm expelling you from this school, no, better yet that's too easy. I'm going to take away something you love first. First, I'll rip you from the band, then I'll prohibit you from lunch, and finally I'll take away your Physical Education course. And if you don't get your act together by then, then I'll expel you from this school. Now, get out of my office!" She huffed and puffed, and blew me out the door.

Wow, this lady really is crazy. She has psychopath written perfectly in the center of her molded face. What she ought to do is get a nose job; the way she looks at people is enough to make me puke.

But, who cares about Dr. Adams? She'll always be a witch, one who will go down in the history books labeled as a Principal Desperate for Attention. Boy, if she was a super hero, and gained her powers by the amount of people she aggravated, she would truly rule the world.

Off to band practice I go. Our football team has

its first game in two weeks. Based on the last three years here, people just come to see the band. So, we have to give the fans a reason to pay their money. I don't know why people pay money to see a sorry football game anyway.

Yeah, yeah I may sound like the one with the sour school spirit, but it's just a game with boys in tights and pads. Sounds like the right fit for a tampon commercial to me. Anyways, it's just a game with boys and a few girls in tights and pads running after a ball made up of the food I eat for breakfast. I mean, how entertaining could such a sport be to watch? Any sport with a ball in my opinion kind of sucks. Balls have no purpose in life and at the end of the day they don't help anybody. However, I am not stupid enough to share my opinion with the Band Director or any Coach.

When I'm in the band I'm able to bring music that speaks to people's hearts and souls, not spoiling it with the sight of a ball going back and forth across the field. With our music, we get to heal lives, bring smiles, get our groove on and most importantly get the ladies. Ladies love a dude that can play the saxophone; you should see the amount of underwear being thrown at me during a halftime performance. At one of our preseason halftime performances, it got so bad that the referee started flagging the girls for unnecessary contact.

Well, actually that's not true, not true at all. But I do believe I could get more girls than any old jock, any day, any time. Just because they're all big and muscular doesn't mean they're all that. And yeah you can say what you want to say, I'm hating on the football players, because I'm tired of them always getting all the beautiful *girls, just because they possess a talent that they don't deserve.*

Band practice is almost over and I'm stuck here trying to figure out all the crap our band director was just saying. I must admit though, I can play the saxophone well, but I have a hard time reading the music, so I pretty much play by ear. Once I've heard the music one time, everything is in place. Now that I think about it, people might say that I have a gift that I don't deserve. Oh well, long as the band director doesn't find out, I'm good. I wonder if my Moms' is coming to practice or going straight home.

I'm so happy I'm sixteen now. I've already got my license and I should be getting my car in two weeks. My Moms' promised to get me a '98 something. I think it's only costing her like twelve hundred bucks. For now, I ride out with my boy Fred who stays about five minutes from me. Fred plays the drums and he's a Junior this year.

I met Fred after my dad had left us; Fred became a role model for me to try to do right and be right no matter what. Fred was always cool till he got into what I call Jesus fest. Fred helped me out a lot, and we got into some trouble big time. There is nothing more I dislike about Fred, than when he goes on those random fast, speaking in tongues and stuff, just driving me crazy!

Looks like I don't see Moms anywhere so I'll just ride back home with Fred. Our homes are about twenty minutes away from the school. Fred and I love to keep the windows down and turn up the music, believe you me, the neighbors know when we come through.

I pretty much hate my neighborhood. With the exception of two or maybe like three people, our neighborhood is full of diaper wearing retirees who don't have anything good to do but complain. You'd think that they'd learn how to do some sewing or bingo playing or something. Just wait till I get my car; they'll probably petition to oust me from the neighborhood. I will play my radio so loud, that even a six-foot seven basketball player could hear it standing up on a ladder.

"Hey, Fred, I appreciate the ride man," I shut the car door.

"No problem J. I'm just about to go home and crash for a minute. I'll call your house to see if you want to play some shooting games later on," he said with a rush of adrenaline.

"Yeah, that's cool man. I ain't got too much work to be doing anyway. How do you think I did in the practice today?" *I feel embarrassed asking him this.*

"I think you was straight, a little off-key, but man you was pretty good overall." *At least he gave me his honest opinion.*

"Alright, Fred, I appreciate it. Holler at you later."

I AM THE DREAM

*"I came to you today, Justin, so you can under-
stand who I Am and then I'll show you who you
make Me out to be. Come, picture this time in your
life Justin: When you were constantly wetting the
bed at five? And didn't know why it was happening? Well, I knew why, I was just waiting on you to
seek Me. After the thirtieth straight day of wetting
your bed, you finally decided to come to Me with
your little prayer, a small quivering voice; but you
had a big heart because you believed that I could
stop it.*

Although I could have immediately stopped
the urinary tract infection, I waited and tested you
for a few more days to see if you still believed.
To My pleasure, you did believe, and you got on
your little knees and prayed to Me at night before
you went to sleep. I was so moved by you, because
that type of belief and will power was not taught
to you at the time, yet you trusted in me, the One
you called your Imaginary Friend. Even the angels
were crying in tears to Me, to see such a presence

and bold act of faith in you. My love for you was so strong till I couldn't contain My healing measure for you anymore. So, there I healed you on the seventh day of prayer.

You thanked Me, loved Me and had brief moments that you mentioned Me, but the passion you possessed for Me had dwindled and all but vanished until the heart break from the fall of your father began to fill you with anger, malice, and hate against Me your Spiritual Father, your true Father and your Creator.

You see Justin; there is a missing piece that you forgot to understand about me. That piece is love. Unless you understand the basic fact that I love you unconditionally: and I decided to give my son Jesus Christ to save you and the rest of the world; then you don't know Me. You don't know Me at all Justin, and the lies you tell your friends about Me, disturbs the very core of my being. Even the very presence of heaven stands still when you choose to curse My name.

There are countless reports of your outlandish behavior against Me Justin, and it continues to reach so high into the heavens, that there is no more room to contain it. Angel after angel would want to destroy you, but I continue to give you grace, mercy and peace, because I love you. How could you spread such hate before Me, if you don't even know Me?

I am Alpha and Omega the beginning and the ending. I am whom some say I am, while many fail to acknowledge that I exist. I am the Master, Creator, and Ruler of all things. I created you in My likeness just as well as those whom have walked, and will walk this Earth. I created all things to give worship unto Me. Even the tiny bees give me praise when they come out in the spring and pollinate the flowers. They give Me praise by simply doing what I made them to do. This world was created for you Justin, and you were created for Me.

When will you get back on fire for Me, not on fire against Me? When will you stop blaspheming my name, and put down those dirty magazines? Be careful what you put in front of the eye gate, for it is the very thing which controls your thoughts, will, and emotions."

"Mama, have you seen my wave cap?" I yelled out.

"No, Justin, and I know what you are doing. You are trying to be late for school again. Boy, I'm not playing with you; you be late again for class and I'm taking you out of band!" She threatens once more.

"Not the first time I heard that," I muttered under my breath, as my mind returned to that weird dream I had last night. I felt like God himself had come down from heaven, entered my head, and took me on a ride. A ride through my life that is. It was shocking at best and scary at most. Maybe I'll call my backsliding father to figure out what the dream meant.

"Justin? Justin, boy do you hear me? Let's

go! We are not going to be late today," my mother gathered her things.

"I'm coming, I'm coming. I just can't find my wave cap," I feel rushed.

"And where's your sister?" My mother asked.

"Why you tripping Ma? You know that she's already left for school. You ok?"

"No, not really, I was thinking about your father this morning," she sighed.

"But I thought you were through with that fool," I reminded her with a pointed look.

"Watch your mouth," she warned. "And you can never be through with a man whose son looks exactly as handsome, charming, and smart like you."

"But I thought that you and buddy were talking about getting married!"

"We are, but we are also talking about the kids we have. He has four. Two of them live with him. He's never been married before, and if you add those two to the bunch along with you and Precious we'll be a family of six."

"That's cool. As long as the brotha' don't try to boss me around and act like he's my father, then we'll be straight." *The last thing I need is another no good father running around here with his pants down.*

"I thought that you two got along well, you said that you liked him," my mother responded back.

"Yeah, with the exception that he doesn't live with us and knowing that the brotha is trying to put his best foot forward to please you, so you can be his wife."

"Good point," my mother smiled at me.

"Mom, what do you think about God?"

"Why did you ask that honey? I think a lot of things about God," she responded nonchalantly.

"It's just that I had this crazy dream. It seemed like God himself just flew down from heaven and entered my head. I felt horrible when I woke up."

"Well son, right now is not the time to talk about God, because I'm sure he doesn't want us to be late for school. But we can talk about God tonight with your future stepfather," she calmed my nerves with a rub on the shoulders.

"Good, maybe he'll side with me on some of my beliefs."

"Don't get me wrong son; I love the Lord and God is a good God, but right now is not the place for such an intimate conversation about the One who loves me more than anyone could ever imagine or describe."

"Did you talk to God last night or something? Because that sounds like something he said?"

"We'll talk it over at dinner tonight at Red Lobster. In the mean time, you and I both have one minute to be in class."

"Alright Ma, I'll see you tonight."

"Actually you'll see me in fourth period, silly."

"Oh, I knew that." I grinned sheepishly.

Off to art class I go. Having to deal with this guy again is driving me crazy. I wish Mrs. Adams would fire him, now that would be worth it. He is boring, sarcastic, and most importantly, a self absorbed moron. Look at him waving his touchy feely hands in the air as if he's trying out for a rewrite to Ghost Busters.

"Ok, class. Welcome to another exciting day of Art! On Monday, we talked about every day art that fills our lives such as the trees, oceans, sky scrapers, practically anything you put your hands on is a work of art, right,
Mr. Lewis?"

There he goes calling me out again, I ought to kick that bastard in a place where it'll really hurt, and see if he'll tell me about the art in that.

"Yeah, yeah, Sir you're right," I said.

"Today we will talk about dreams. Where do dreams come from? How do dreams bring to life all that coexists?"

Wow what the heck is going on? Did God tell him about the dream as well? Am I just starting to go crazy? Wait a minute, was that really a dream, or am I just imaging things? Let's see what this guy has to say about dreams.

"Dreams are the subtle beauty of life's vast imaginations. They give us a chance of hope, love, faith, survival, and most importantly, a chance to live our lives beyond our physical existence. If you have been abducted by an alien, wounded in combat, swam with the octopus and seen God from

Mars, then guess what folks? You have had a dream," the teacher chuckled.

"Now, not to debunk any religious folk or individuals who have been abducted by aliens, but I believe that dreams, in its entirety my friends, are the true secrets of what lies in the life ahead and the edifice of past memories.

Many of you may ask, 'What do dreams have to do with art?' Well students, dreams have everything to do with art. Mr. Lewis, I see you're actually paying attention to me today. Please, tell me what did you dream about last night? And no X-rated material by the way." The teacher gestured for me to answer.

Why does this guy continue to embarrass me in front of this class? He loves and lives to pick on me. He wouldn't be happy go lucky if I went up there and swung on him. I really don't think he gets it. So what should I do God? Should I tell him the truth or a lie? I mean, I don't want to be embarrassed if I said that God came to me in a dream last night. They'll be ready to throw me in with the other crazies walking around the school. But I bet that's what you want me to do, God. You want me to tell the truth.

"Mr. Lewis we are sitting here bored and waiting." The teacher looked around jokingly.

He's got some nerves. "I--- had a dream about God last night. As a matter of fact, God himself came to me in my dream. It was like the strangest thing," The class looked at me with eyes of astonishment, humor, and some tinged with fear. But I didn't care what they thought; I had to talk about this great encounter.

"So God was rolling up in a Cadillac riding on twenty-two's, he had Jesus to the left and somebody else to the right. He told me that I needed to get my act together or it's gone be hard times for me. Then he pointed out the demons on the side with gold grills in their mouths, waiting to eat me up. Then as the hydro started pumping, I seen a bright white angel underneath the car and Jesus said that angel was waiting for me."

"Mr. Lewis, Mr. Lewis you can stop right there," my teacher shook his head in frustration. "For one, your dream is absolutely ludicrous, and two, that's quite an insult to the Christian belief, and all those who choose to worship God as Master. Do you have anything to say for yourself?"

"Yeah, I only wanted to make people laugh because everybody started looking at me strange." I hope he doesn't give me an F.

"But, Justin." Right then when he called my name, it sounded as if God himself said it.

"Justin did you really have a dream about God last night? Please tell your class and yourself the truth." The teacher is looking at me now with a blank stare. *You would have thought that I was the Anti-Christ with that look he gave me.*

"Yes, I did have a dream about God last night, Sir. He told me about how when I was a kid I got on my knees and prayed to him constantly. I prayed to him to heal a urinary infection that I had. This is kind of embarrassing but I was just peeing in the bed constantly when I was five years. He told me that He loved my commitment and faithfulness to Him. I must say, since I had that dream about Him last night, my opinion of Him is a lot different from what most people I know, see Him as.

Although God seemed to be sturdy and firm in his words, I still felt a sense of loving, caring, and expectation to be the best person I can be. It felt like he was my father. Well this may sound cheesy to say this, but he's father to all of us. God came to me in a dream last night and I am no longer ashamed to talk about it. I realized that although I have my dirt and many times I have cursed his name. I realized that the God I seen last night is not ashamed of me. You can say whatever you want to say but that's just how I feel. I'm going to sit down now; I don't have time for this."

The classroom broke out in a thunderous applause for me. I mean it was loud, I'm sure my mom's class room down the hall could hear the clapping. It was so loud that one of the security guards came in running thinking there was a fight. I was so overwhelmed that I ran out the class, fighting back tears. The professor came out behind me.

"Son, today is the beginning of a new day for you, don't let this moment be forgotten. I'm proud of you, Mr. Lewis. You were brave today. Now, let's go back inside, we have an assignment to talk about."

"Well, what's the assignment?" I asked.

"We will talk about it in class. Come on." He gave me what I thought was his first real smile. *I hope this man don't have anything else for me to do; I don't think I can break down like that again.*

"Students, your assignment for tonight is to draw from your perspective on Mr. Lewis dream. There is no right or wrong way to do it. I want you to draw in detail what he said and we'll discuss it next class. Here is your chance to give your visual interpretation of a dream. Let his dream become your dream."

I AM THE MIRACLE

"You know, Mom, it's been a while since we've been out to eat, especially at a place like Red Lobster. What's the occasion?"

"Don't trip, Justin. I told you this morning that we were going out to eat. Besides, it was Rick's suggestion."

Glaring at Rick I say, "Well how come Precious couldn't come? She would've loved Red Lobster."

"I know baby, but Rick wanted to have a one on one with the three of us. And next week when Precious, Rick and I go to the barbecue joint, you won't be there. I know that your sister loves barbecue, and I know this is your favorite restaurant. So relax, chill, and let's just have a good night."

Oh I'm having a good night; I can't wait to tell her about what happened to me in school today. Let me leave out the part about me crying in school though. I don't want Rick to think I'm a punk or something. Just when I was about to speak, the waitress interrupts.

"Hello, how may I serve you all tonight? Are there any more guests to be expected?" I swear the girl of my dreams just stepped before my very eyes: *Beautiful brown eyes, light on the weight, and a girl next door attitude you'd start a fundraiser for. Who the heck cares if she might be a few years older than me?*

Oh God, I want this one. Give her to me now! I'll get on my knees at the bar if she even gives me a hint of interest. She just winked at me. Ok, ok time for me to get up and fulfill the promise I made to God.

"Justin, what you doing baby?" My mother looked toward me.

"Um, I got to go to the bathroom right quick." *Now that's sad, I just told a lie to save my Mom or myself the embarrassment, so she won't stop me from going to the bar.*

As I rush on over to the bar, I take a quick peek of all the people around me, then I sink to my knees for a quick ten seconds, and then scurry back up with eyes looking at me as if I played the starring role in the Exorcist. I brush them off and then head back to my seat. Luckily for me, mom was so into Rick that they didn't even notice the event. The waitress noticed, and asked me if I was on my knees for religious purposes.

I said no, explaining that I was just fulfilling a promise I made to God. She winked at me again and again and again till I noticed that she actually has a blinking problem. She wasn't winking at me at the table because she desired to be with me. She was winking at me because she just couldn't help it. "God that's not fair," I muttered under my breath.

Then, just like in my dream, He spoke softly right back to me and said, **"You created your own path, I just let it happen. Now you know what it feels like to make a promise to me, and be faithful and prudent to act on it. I rejoice with you this day for that."**

And just as quickly as his voice spoke, it was gone, leaving an imprint on my mind and heart.

"So, Justin, do you feel better now?" *Wait a minute. How does she know* about it?

"Feel better about what?" I asked my mom, feeling so wrapped up with guilt inside.

"Feel better about going to the restroom? Do I actually have to spell it out? I mean, that *is* where you went right?"

"Honey, honey its ok. The boy is sixteen years old, Sandra. I'm sure he doesn't feel like talking about how he feels when he leaves the restroom." Rick intervened.

"Yeah, you're right Ricky, I took it too far Justin. Do you know what you would like to eat yet, Justin?"

"Yeah, I'll get the coconut shrimp with the salmon and french fries. Here comes the waitress now. I'll just tell her."

"Here are your drinks. Wow you must be proud mam," the waitress beamed.

Oh no, she's about to tell, she's about to tell.

My mom looked curiously at the waitress

and said, "Proud of what?"

"Your son. Well, he's such a handsome guy a cutie pie if you ask me," she blushed.

I hit my head on the table after that comment.

"Hey, Justin, you ok?" My mother questioned.

"Yes, yes I'm ok. I just can't believe my ears."

"How old are you young lady?" My mother quizzed her.

"I just turned nineteen." The waitress said with a smile.

"You are too old for my Justin." My mother hinted with a voice of both sarcasm and disappointment.

"Yeah, I know." The waitress sighed.

"How do you know?" My mother flipped out.

"He's still got that cute baby face," the waitress complemented.

"Are you some kind of sexual predator that we need to know about? I mean, Alicia, right? You are three years older than him. What the heck do you plan on doing with my son?" My mother's voice rose above the chatter, causing eyes to flicker her way.

"I-- I'm sorry I said anything. I just think he's cute a-- and, maybe one day he and I could go out," the waitress stuttered.

"Well, I hate to break your heart sista, but that day will be a long while from now. I am a high school teacher and I see cases like this all the time,"

My mother's tone was laced with accusation.

My Mom is really tripping right now; all the girl wants to do is have a conversation with me. What can be wrong with that? I gots to say something to calm my Moms down. Uh-oh. Slick Rick is about to say something.

"Sweetheart, calm down and give the girl a chance, she just wants to talk to the boy, not make love," Rick reasoned.

"Rick, since when did you get in the business of taking up for Justin?" My mother scorned him.

"You know what ladies and gentlemen? I'll be back," said Alicia, as she backed away and fled from the table.

"I'm not trying to tell you how to raise your son, Sandra, but he's a boy. For all we know he could be dating women your age," he pointed out. "At least she had the guts to come up to you and tell you what she thought. All you had to do was listen and then later on talk it over with Justin. I mean, look at the boy; he's drooling like a virgin on Saturday Night Live.

"You're right again, Rick, and I'm sorry for the assumption. I just don't want my son to be hurt." My mother turned to me. "So what do you think of all this Justin?"

"I like her. I really, really like her. As a matter of fact, I lied about going to the bathroom. When I first laid eyes on Alicia, my mind was like: that's the one for me. So, I made a promise to God that if she would even wink at me, I'd go to the bar on my knees. Needless to say, she did wink, and I was at the bar on my knees looking stupid. But I felt like I had to do it because I made a promise to God. As much as I don't really know about God, I just felt like it was something I had to do," I confessed.

"Ok, Justin I forgive you for lying." My mother turned to Rick. "See I know my son. Now that you mentioned God, let's talk about Him. You asked me earlier what did I think about God, and I told you that we'd discuss it with you. So here you are. Let's talk."

Here comes Alicia again. "Here is your food, folks, let me know if I can be of any assistance. Would any of you like a refill?"

"Well, first off, Alicia, I'm sorry the way I came at you. I'm just very protective of my two children, that's all." My mother calmly apologized.

"That's understandable M'am," Alicia responded with a humbled tone.

"Call me Sandra," my mother insisted.

"That's understandable Sandra, I think I just came off a little too friendly. I really don't know what that was. I'm not usually that forward," Alicia confessed with those beautiful eyes.

"It's ok dear. Thanks for the food." My mother insisted.

Now can we get back to the story, I feel like I'm going to explode.

"Do you have a card on you Alicia, where we could call you?" said my outrageously wrong mother. I mean, I barely spoke to the girl, and here my mom is asking for her number, that's my job. Now I really feel like I'm younger than her.

"No, I don't have a card, but here's my number, I'll write it on a napkin for you," Alicia scribbled furiously and handed the napkin to my mother before taking off.

"This food smells good, will you bless us with the grace, Rick?"

"Sure, my love. Dear God, I thank you for the many blessings you have brought upon our lives. I thank you for both the good and the bad. Lord, I thank you for this moment we have right now." My mother nudges him on the side to signal for him to hurry up with the grace. "Thank you for this food that we are about to eat for the nourishment of our bodies. In Jesus name. Amen."

Amen to that, I thought that Rick was about to bring down the Angels with his grace. At least God knows he's grateful.

"Justin what's wrong with you, baby? You not hungry anymore?"

"No Ma, I'm just thinking." *Thinking about that dime piece, Alicia.*

"About that girl, Alicia?" She immediately assumed.

"No, I'm thinking about God. I mean, it seems like quite a miracle the way it all went down. Do you think that God matches people? Like, does he put certain people together for a certain reason?" I shared with them in my enthusiasm.

"Of course God matches up people. He's the

biggest match maker of them all. Look how he matched up Adam with Eve. Although they fell in sin, the two were ultimately perfect for each other, and you and I wouldn't be here today if God did not think other wise. Adam could have said 'oh she's too skinny,' or 'I can't be with her,' or 'she's just not my type so I don't want to have kids with her.' Imagine right then and there the first people being the last."

"Wow, I never thought about it like that; that's kind of dope."

"Why do you think Rick and I get along so well, we're a perfect match, well, at least, almost?" She hesitated.

"What about you and dad? Did God mess up when he brought you two together?" *I can tell she felt a little uncomfortable when I mentioned him, I shouldn't have brought it up.*

"No baby, God did not mess up. He did just fine; your father messed up. You see, God can give us the perfect partner, like your girl, Alicia for example. But it's up to us to keep that individual. Certain things such as cheating can ruin what God made for good, so that's why your dad and I have separated.

Let me tell you something, Justin, never think that it is your fault or Precious fault that we broke up. It was his fault, right Rick?" My mother looked over to Rick.

"Hey I'm just listening right now, Baby," Rick patted my mom on the shoulders.

"Listen, Justin. When you asked me about

God earlier today, I had a flash of so many memories. One particular memory was of a young man by the name of Edward. Boy, did he sweep me off my feet my senior year in high school. He was a devout Christian, and my first love. He wanted to be a dentist."

"Well what happened to him, Ma? I mean, it would be nice if you shared these kinds of things with us more often." A few tears fell down my mother's face; she looked down and then looked back up and said, "He died while visiting his home land of Haiti. Word had it, that Edward was praying over this voodoo doctor and the voodoo doctor killed him. It's too traumatic to describe the rest of what went on.

At that moment Justin, I had very mixed feelings about God. I was constantly asking why him, why he took my Edward. Until I remembered the sweet soft words spoken to me by Edward himself. All the scriptures he read to me, all the times he treated me so good, and since that day I've been trying to find my Edward, the spirit of love that lived in him. I had in the back of my mind that his spirit will always live on in my life.

I thought that your father was my Edward. At first he seemed to do and be everything right. After we had Precious, a lot of things changed, and I started seeing a different side to your father.

I don't want to continue talking about your father or Edward while we're here with Rick, but I must say that I think I've found my Edward again.

I found my Edward in Rick. When you love some-body, Justin, you can never let go of the memories of that person both good and bad. Although you may let go of the person, it's very rare that you'll let go of the ideals and standards that made you love that person in the first place. Even when you decide to search for another mate, that past lover will still stick to you like glue. Right, Rick?"

"Right, well speaking of love we have dessert coming out."

"Why are the waiters singing Rick?" My mom looked Rick up and down.

"I don't know, but it looks like that slice is specifically for you."

"Is it?" My mom said.

"Oh, yes," said Rick.

"What is that on top, looking all shiny and definitely inedible?" My mom's eyes are bulging out with pure surprise and shock.

Oh boy he's going to pop the big question, but why did he have to do this tonight? Couldn't he have waited twenty more years? I'll be sure to be out the house by then! These waiters and waitresses sure can't carry a tune. I think he hired the wrong cast to make a proposal.

On one knee Ricky goes. "Baby it's time; we've been seeing each other for two years. We stayed pure and even made sure we didn't call each other after a certain time. Right now I'm ready to break the barriers, because you know what, we won't get any younger. So Sandra, would you do me the honor of being my wife?"

Mom is just balking up crying at this point. She is in full surprise mode. She can't believe her heart. She can't catch her breath from the excitement. With a simple nod of yes, Rick takes the ring off the cake and puts it on her ring finger. Now the whole restaurant is clapping for joy as I spot Alicia looking at me like a deer caught in headlights.

I'm looking back at her, feeling kind of lucky like Rick, and ready to find me a ring to put on her finger. Let me stop dreaming. I've got a while to go, I'm only sixteen. I wish Precious was here, she'd be crying right along with Mama. Wow, I can't believe my very eyes. Let me call Precious. What just happened tonight and today and today and tonight? Whatever just happened is truly a miracle.

I AM THE WAY MAKER

"Have you thought about how much the wedding is going to cost yet, Rick?" My mother enquired.

"No, not yet, I need to first figure out how many people are supposed to be there. I mean do you want a small, medium, or large wedding?" Rick passionately asked.

"I just want a simple wedding, baby. The last thing I want is for us to go bankrupt before we even say I do." My mother reasoned.

"I know, don't worry about it, we got a whole nine months to think about this thing," Rick assured her, extending his hand out to my mother.

"Baby, nine months is not a whole lot of time when you're talking about a wedding, there is so much planning included. Everything has to be perfect," My mother settled into Rick's arms.

"Don't worry; every thing is going to be fine. Just think, in nine months you'll be Mrs. Sandra Rome."

"I like that, I like that, but how are we even going to afford it? I am way behind on bills, plus Justin and Precious seem to need something new every week."

"Sandra I know, I know, remember; I have two kids as well. Hey, just like God brought us together, the Lord will make a way for us. He will provide all of our needs and he's also going to pay for the honeymoon." *Now that's what makes the wedding worth it, the honeymoon. Can't wait for mine!*

"Very funny! You watch buddy, the clock is ticking." My mother giggles over the hot stove. Hope she doesn't get burned.

"You watch, you will be amazed at what God can do." Rick told my mother as he pulled the God card once more.

"You sound so confident." Sandra puts down the pot and looks at him.

"I serve a confident God and so do you. You should feel the same way I do." Rick assured her.

"I know, I know Rick; I'm just a little nervous, jittery, and kind of intoxicated with happiness."

"Well, happiness always sounds good to me baby. Hey, I have to get back to work, so I'll call you later and we'll talk some more about this. Ok?"

"Yeah, hey wait a minute Rick."

"What?" Rick turned around and faced my mother.

"Thanks for being so positive about everything, I really needed that. You know how us girls can be, gone with the whirl wind, thinking about every worst possibility there is."

"Baby, it was nothing. You know I'm here for you," he leaned over and gave my mother a kiss on the cheeks.

"You sure you don't want any of this spaghetti I made for you," my mom suggested.

"No, I'm good, I need to get home and see the kids. But I don't mind taking a plate home. If that's alright with you?" My mother took a quick pause and said, "Baby you can take me home if you like."

"Sandra I wish I could, but we are only a few months away, so I know we can keep our purity before God for this marriage."

With a sad look of disapproval my mother said, "Oh well, here's your food, and have a good night."

"So tell me all about how Rick proposed to mom; Justin."
"It's too much to describe. You just had to be there, Precious; you had to be there."

"I heard that you met this girl that is supposed to be in love with you. I mean what's up with you and mom? Did the love bug hit you two and pass me by? I want somebody to love me, I want somebody to write me sweet poems and give me wet kisses," Precious sighed dreamily.

"Hey, you are too young for that. What kind of love are you looking for in the seventh grade? Mom loves you, I love you, and Dad loves you too," I pushed her playfully.

"I'm not talking about that Justin, I'm talking about being able to date a boy, talk to him on the phone and listen to him read me poems all night long. It's not like I want to do other things like the other girls do," Precious rolled her eyes heavenward. *Oh boy I think I already know the answer to this, and probably don't want to know, but since I'm big brother I have to listen anyway.*

"You know, you know Justin, the other girls do stuff with guys in the bathroom, in the back of the portable or in the back of the bus," Precious informed me.

"What kind of stuff are you talking about Precious?" *I really don't want to hear this; my little sister doesn't need to know anything about sex.*

"They... kind of touch each others body parts and stuff. Sometimes I even see some of them deep kissing," Precious confessed, clearly embarrassed about what she just admitted to me.

"Have you ever seen a guy naked?"

"No." She rolled her eyes at me.

"So you're still a virgin?" *I figured that was the easiest way to get that answer out of her.*

"No duh, Justin! Mom would *kill* me if she thought that I wasn't; every week she checks me down there to make sure something is not broken she says. I *hate* that mom checks me like that. Makes

43

me feel like she doesn't trust me; can you get her to stop that for me Justin?"

"This is my first time hearing about that between you and mom; I'll make sure to speak to her about it." *This kind of talk makes me very uncomfortable; I would feel like a fool talking to my mother about Precious female issues.*

"Besides, it's not like I want to have sex right now anyways. I think however it feels, it's got to be overrated. Because from what I hear from the girls that have done it, all of them said that their boyfriends didn't act the same after it happened. Most of them said they were miserable, while a few girls actually talked about suicide. Are *you* still a virgin Justin?"

"Of course not, I lost my virginity when I was fourteen." *Oops I said that too quick. I should have waited and maybe said it a little differently. Hope I don't give my little sister any bad ideas.*

"Well I'm going to wait until I'm married; Mom said that's the best thing to do."

"And mom was definitely right by telling you that." *At least my little sister's got her head on straight. It's amazing how this world works. I can feel free to mess with somebody's little sister, but when it comes down to my little sister I don't want to hear it. That's so crazy. Oh well, its not like I made the three girls I've been with have sex with me. They chose to do it with me like I chose them.*

Anyway, enough about my sex life. This is actually a moment when I can't wait to get to art class. Maybe one of those interpretations of my dream will give me an answer.

"Hey lil sis, lunch is almost over, so I have to hang up the phone. I'll see you later tonight; we have a very long band practice today because we have a big game coming up tomorrow night."

"Justin, since when you started rushing off the phone for class? I thought your break wasn't over till you get a detention," Precious jogged her memory.   "Well today is different. I'll tell you all about it when I get home tonight."

"Ok, bye."

"Mr. Lewis, I am very surprised to see you here on time. Was the cafeteria food that bad today?" The art teacher suffered through the laughter of the students. "No sir, I'm just here to make a difference. I want to be a better student."

"You sure its not just because the whole class did work based on you?" *That's it. Why else would I want to come to this phony baloney class?*

"Yeah pretty much, I guess that's it," I said flippantly.

"Share the truth the next time you waltz in early Mr. Lewis. You're starting to smell like a liar. Go have your seat now. Class, today we will begin our artistic journey on the idealism that all art is good art. Can somebody explain to the class why that is?"

Of course Nancy would raise her hands; she thinks she's so smart. To me she's very beautiful, so I'll leave that alone. I tried to talk to the girl one day, boy did she give me a dead president. That look was one in a million. Here she goes, yap pity, yap yapping. Now that I think about it, how could I have her for a girlfriend? Not only does she talk too much, but she's clearly high maintenance.

"And you're right, Nancy," said our teacher. "Art is clearly seen in the eye of the beholder, so there never could be a right or wrong way to do it. As both an artist and teacher I have seen some of the most devastating pieces to ever be captured by the human eye. I mean they were just flat ugly to me class. Those same devastating pieces that looked so ugly to me, sold for fifty thousand a piece at an auction in Chicago. When I heard the news of that, I almost fainted.

There I was with three drawings, very beautiful drawings of the sky which captured the audience, and I barely made one thousand dollars on all three put together. You can never tell by going to those shows what the people with money or influence would like. As a matter of fact, because of a lack of money, I turned to teaching. The art market is very precarious.

So, someone answer this question: If money was never an issue, what would be your motivation to live? Alex, since you've raised your hand first, you can go ahead."

This is boring I thought the class was going to be about me today. Instead he wants to talk about not making enough money. Screw that, I'm about to jet.

"And Mr. Lewis, where do you think you're going?"

"I'm going to the bathroom."

"Without my permission?" *What up with the art teacher questioning me like this.*

"Yeah, that's right, without your permission."

"I must tell you Mr. Lewis I know your kind like a book: you want everything to be about *you*." *What does he mean your kind? That's ok I'll pass on that statement.*

"When you can't get all the attention focused on you, then you break down and leave." He lectured me.

"I said I was going to the bathroom!"

"No, Mr. Lewis. You were going to skip the rest of the class. Is that the truth Mr. Lewis?"

This guy does know me like a book. He must talk to my Mom everyday. "Yes, that's the truth, sir. I just got tired of all that nonsense. I wanted to see what everybody thought of my dream. I'm trying to find some answers and it doesn't seem like I can get them soon enough," I admitted.

"You will get them my dear friend, just as soon as you sit down, relax and breathe. What you fail to realize Mr. Lewis is that today's class has been about you this whole time. What you think of as a mediocre, or illogical conversation, is really about how to show the many interpretations of your dreams at a gallery or two. And you know what else? We may just sell them to raise funds for our class.

Now, wouldn't that be nice, Mr. Lewis?

Wouldn't it be nice to know that the vision you gave each one of our students is now used in a tangible form to show the world your dream from God? Class, show Mr. Lewis how you interpreted his dream." The veils were pulled down, and everything that was once thought impossible, has now become possible.

Wow, they are so beautiful. I don't think I've ever seen anything like this, and not one painting is the same. As each student comes before me, I feel like I'm about to cry again.

"You see here, Mr. Lewis; through all your huffing and puffing, right here is the dream you started and shared for us all to visualize. Go ahead, you can cry, because God will wipe your teary eyes. In the end, all you need to know is that the Lord will make a way. Class dismissed."

I AM THE TRUTH

"So what happened today, Justin? What was so exciting that made you hang up the phone during lunch?" Precious interrogated me.

"It is unexplainable, Precious, unexplainable. It's been some things happening to me these past few days that are kind of creeping me out. I mean you pretty much know how I feel about God, right?"

"Yeah who doesn't, you feel that's he's just some sort of mystical being that every parent tells their kid about so they can feel safe. You always love to say that you can't trust something you can't see. And usually the things you can't see are evil. And of course you love to continue on with your ranting, so pretty much I know your whole script. Why? Why do you ask? You think that He's even less than what you talk about Him being."

"No, He's more," I assured my sister Precious.

"Now wait a minute here Justin, I know I didn't hear that coming out of my big brothers mouth," she examined my every expression.

"Yes, I feel that God is more and that's what's

been bothering me these past few days. He came to me in a dream, Precious; he came to me in a dream," I pleaded my case to her.

"Well, how do you know that was God, and not you just imagining a whole bunch of stuff?" Precious rose her eyebrows in curiosity.

"I know that I know because He brought up some things in my life that I clearly forgot, and I was just blown away by His presence. It felt sort of magnetic. Why am I telling you this? You're too young for me to talk to you about this."

"Too young? Oh, so I'm too young to talk about this but not about sex?"

Whoops that's a bite in the foot. She does have a point, but I'd really rather not talk about this anymore. "Well, I feel kind of burnt out from a long day."

"Ok, but I'm not giving up on your new found beliefs."

"It's not new found beliefs, Precious; I've always believed that there was a God, just not to the extent that I kind of do now," I tried to kindly get her to understand my view point, as she is over there smiling to no end.

"Have you talked to Mom about this?"

"Mom, Ricky, and I talked a little about this at Red Lobster where I met that girl Alicia. I'm going to give Alicia a call tonight."

"Do you plan on doing bad things to her?" She looked at me with complete sincerity.

"Of course not; just have a friendly conversation that's all. Mom doesn't like it because Alicia's a few years older than me."

"How come you always get to find some-body?"

Oh no, here we go again, this girl is going to bug me about boys for the rest of her life. I almost want to say, go out there get you a boyfriend and find out what we can be like; but I know that I would get in trouble if I said that. So I will just be the big brother that I am and tell her differently.

"Listen, Precious. I don't want to have this conversation about you dating boys. When mom says you can date which will probably be at about sixty-five, then we'll talk. So, since we have another fifty-three years to go, let's keep it on the hush-hush." I laughed at her so hard.

"Stop picking on me. Mom says that when my prince lands on the porch after I turn eighteen with a job, good credit and a house, then I'll be able to marry him."

Good luck finding that. Yep it'll be sixty-five. What mom really meant is her Prince will be rolling in on a wheel chair, on Medicaid, taking prescriptions and living off of social security. That sounds like the good life to me; at least he doesn't have to work.

"Here comes Mom," said Precious.

"Mom doesn't look so happy," I told Precious. She looks like a loaded pistol ready to be fired. Let me go to the back and pretend to be doing my home-work. "Precious go clean up the bathroom. I'm going to my room. Mom looks pissed."

"Okay," she ran off.

Here she comes about to walk through the door; let me get lost quick.

"Justin and Precious, come help me with these groceries, sweeties. Justin, stop pretending to do homework and Precious I know that you just started cleaning up the bathroom. You two have been using that trick since elementary school. Come help your Mom with these groceries."

I know I shouldn't have used that one, I should have done the performance where I was washing dishes and Precious sits in the living room watching TV. "I'm coming, I'm coming!" I said as I met my Mom with a kiss and a hug. Precious strolled right behind me as we walked outside to the car and gathered up a few bags.

"What's the occasion, mom?" I asked her.

"We're having Rick over tonight for dinner, we have to go over a few plans for the wedding, so we thought it would be good to include the both of you in our decision making. Don't worry, Precious, we are still going to have a separate dinner with you, Me and Rick. Time to clean up this place for real; Rick's coming over in about two hours."

"What you cooking, mama?" I questioned her, while trying to take a sneak peek in the bags.

"I'll be baking chicken tonight with a little barbecue sauce, carrots, broccoli, red wine and your favorite, Justin." *Wonder what that is.*

"What's that?"

"Sweet potato cornbread."

That is my favorite, I love some sweet potato

cornbread. Mom makes it taste so good. Especially when she melts that butter on top when it's done. It's both a desert and main course for me. I can't wait till it's ready.

"I hope you cook enough for the week," I told my mom.

"That's if you don't eat it all today, baby?"

"Hey Ma, since you're inviting Rick over, do you mind if I invite Alicia?" "Now, Son, not only is that out of the question but I think that is selfish on your part. I'm not real comfortable with you being with that girl. But you know what, Justin? You children are going to do what you do anyway, so I'm going to leave that part alone. And no, she can't come over for dinner."

Mom knows me like a book; she knew I would ask a second time just to see if she would budge just a little. Anyways, let me get back to cleaning up this house before she starts swinging that belt around. Ever since Daddy left, she has no problem showing us she can wear the pants in the family. As a matter of fact she whipped that belt out so much, I ran when I just heard the sound of it blazing across the hallway into my room.

"Justin, stop day dreaming, Baby. That girl's already got your hormones running a hundred miles per hour. And wait a minute Mister Playa, Playa. I thought you were already seeing somebody!"

"You're right; I've seen her for a couple of months and now the presentation is over. Come on, Ma, its high school. Nine months with someone is considered a marriage, six you're engaged and three months, well three months is a little bit between

knowing the person and looking for their replace-
ment."

"That Alicia girl is no high school student,
Justin. She's going to be looking for a long term commitment out of you," My mother showed a sense of
concern.

"For her, I'll make an exception," I joked.

"Son, you need to quit. Being in a relationship takes more than a visual fantasy, Justin. you
have to learn to stay true to a woman. You have
to be pure in heart, make her laugh, read her stories and bed side poems like your Dad read to me.
You have to make her feel more important than
the President of the United States. That's how Rick
makes me feel. He will freeze time for me if he
could, just so I can express my inner most thoughts
and feelings, about life, love or whatever."

"Mom, that's deep, but I'm only sixteen. I
think I'll handle it well." She looks like she's ready
to burst into tears; *I knew I should have started cleaning while I had the chance.*

"There is a lot I did at sixteen, Justin, most of
which I am not proud of. Yet, I feel a since of inner
strength when I look back at my moments of sin and
iniquity."

"Mom, what are you talking about?" *She's
starting to sound like she has some kind of confessions
to make. I'm not sure if I want to hear them.*

"Don't worry about it baby. Just get back to
cleaning, forget I even said something about my
past to you. Hurry up; we have thirty minutes till

Rick arrives, I'm not even half way done with cooking. Make sure your sister is doing what she needs to do and stop day dreaming."

I'm assuming that it's Rick at the door, so I'm sure Mom is rushing to get the door as it chimes. I see Precious running out of her room to the door, so I'll follow her lead.

Here mom comes, she opens the door, and there standing in front of us with a white dress shirt, black dress pants and a black tie, is a vacuum cleaner salesman trying to sell us a vacuum cleaner. Mom had to say she wasn't interested at least five times, till he finally left and went on to the neighbor's house. Not too soon after he leaves, Rick shows up, the love of my mother's life. Her face changed so quick you would of thought she was stung by a bee and had an allergic reaction.

Rick comes in the house strutting like he owns it, talking smack and telling me who's going to win the Super Bowl, telling me why my team, the Jaguars, are sorry and will never be anything. Rick is just straight dogging my team. But I really don't care; I'm first and foremost all about the band. Like I said before, I don't think that men running around with tights hitting each other is indication of any real talent or creativity. Rick can talk all he wants, I think it's hilarious.

"So, Sandra, have you told them yet?" said Rick.

"No, not really. Well here it is," My mother turned to face us. "Justin, Precious we want you two to be apart of the whole planning and make up of our wedding."

As if life is not hard enough. I don't want to be apart of planning anything. I'm happy for my mom and all, but I got Alicia on my mind.

"So what do you two think?" My mother asked.

"Great, great," I said. *I know when she heard that, she knew I wasn't enthusiastic about it at all. Maybe if she sees that I'm uninterested, then she'll let me off the hook.*

"How do *you* feel about this Precious?"

"I feel real good about it. It almost feels like I'm going to help plan my own wedding. It's going to be beautiful. Yeah, I can already imagine the colors."

"Wait a minute, Baby; we haven't gotten that far yet. But go ahead and let me know what you think," my mother stopped her in her tracks.

"I would like something like red and white. I can see you with a red wedding dress on, and Rick with a nice white tux. The whole place would look like Valentine's Day, with hearts and kisses, and candles all around. Wow it looks so beautiful as I see it."

"I am ecstatic. I can see the vision as well, Precious. Do you see it Rick?" My mother turned to the stunned Rick.

"Well, I was thinking more like blue and black, but, honey, if you love red and white then lets go with that. You know what they say, the marriage is for the Bride and the honeymoon is for the Groom."

I wonder what Rick was thinking to say that. *Personally I think that marriage sucks, being with one woman for the rest of your life is like being in jail with a lot of privileges. I'd rather just be locked up than to go out on work release, all to end up back at the same place.*

Who came up with this marriage thing anyway? Was it God? Or was it just some scam created by the man in order to get rich off of folks in divorce court? Marriage just sucks!

"You're right Rick, but if the Bride doesn't feel comfortable with the decision making skills of the Groom, then there will be no honeymoon," My mother schooled him confidently.

And the trap begins. I think Rick is thinking what I'm thinking by the way he's looking at me. He's probably saying to himself, 'Lord what did I get myself into?' If I was God, I'd probably tell him that he got himself into a lifetime worth of mess and misery. Not to say that my Moms is bad or anything, but at times she could be just like any old nagging hag.

I remember one day she was trying to teach Precious and I the birds and the bees. That woman talked us to sleep in front of a good chocolate cake. I was so tired of listening to my Mama that I was too tired to take a bite of that fresh chocolate cake. All I wanted to tell her was get to the point, but no, she had to run on with make believe children's stories. I mean it's a simple concept: Man and woman gets overwhelmed by their hormones, Man shoots for the moon and Woman catches him before he falls. Then nine months later, the Woman shoots out a star.

Now that made me realize something; out of the thousands of sperm a man has, he is able to produce one unique child out of the bunch. First there was me, then came Precious. Is this some kind of coincidence, or is it the kind of stuff that God was trying to tell me in my dream? Stuff like he shaped, molded me and knew me before I even left the womb. If you ask me, that's some scary stuff. I mean, how can somebody know exactly how you would come out? Only if the person was like some kind of clone or something, then I could understand. That's just too much stuff to think about. The truth is, only God knows the truth about me and I guess I'm going to have to change my opinions about Him to figure out exactly what He was saying. He definitely didn't have to bring up the peeing incident. Totally uncalled for!

I am swinging so far to the left it's not even funny, talking about this marriage thing is making me think about some stuff I ain't ever thought of before. Some things I don't think I want to know about. All I want to know is the truth. Why did God choose this time to come to my dream? That's all I really care about.

I'm happy my mom is having a wedding, not too concerned about Precious boyfriend questions, and well, hopefully me and Alicia can get married my way. You know, the kind where lovers do the fling without the ring. That's the best policy for me. That way, I'll never have to worry about her taking my half, and at this point, she would only get a slice of my TV. That's the only thing I own and bought with my own money. The truth of the matter is this; what we will be has already been *done. That's what my Daddy use to say back in the day.*

I AM THE OIL

Sometimes when it comes down to finding self, it takes a long time to find that person that lives in you. Things have been going crazy for me these past few weeks. Two months from now, I'll be turning seventeen, heading to my junior year in high school. Sometimes being young can be both a blessing and a curse. With the many pretty girls strutting around and hormones pumping at an all time high, no wonder we teenagers get into a lot of trouble.

I remember this one Saturday night there was this girl that was giving me 'The Look'. She just looked at me and right then and there I knew that she wanted more than just a look at the stars. I thought about walking over to her for a quick minute, but I couldn't. Was that God who stopped me? Or was it just a small piece of my conscience telling me she might have an STD? I didn't even know who the chick was or where she came from. But for whatever reason I just couldn't do it. God knows I was ready, but I guess that night was not the night.

What makes me want to do it so much is the very

fact that aside from school and band practice ain't nothing else going on around here. Everybody's doing it and if you ask me, it feels real good. I hope Alicia isn't one of those chicks who say they can't give up the goods because of their religion. If I can recall correctly, God made sex, and from what I read everything he made is good so that obviously means sex included.

I'm not trying to say that all I want to do is have sex with Alicia and leave, that's not it at all. I'm just saying that if we are to be boyfriend and girlfriend, then she's got to be willing to give up the goods every now and then. How could she say she loves me, but be afraid to share it intimately with me, how whack is that? It's like Rick proposing to my mom and she tells him that he can't get any on their wedding night. I'd be highly pissed, uh let me stop talking about my Moms and Rick, kind of gives me the creeps. Disgusting to think about, might I add?

Boring, boring, boring right now! There comes a point in life when the television is too lame to watch, the internet is too repetitive, and playing basketball with friends is too competitive. So I'll call up my new friend, my new pal, my new something.

"Hello, can I speak to Alicia please?" I said to some dude huffing and puffing on the phone. The brother sounds like he just did the one hundred yard dash and someone forgot to tell him to breathe.

"Who this?" He answered with an attitude.

"This is Justin, who is this?" I shouldn't have asked who he was; now I know I'm in for some trouble.

"It ain't none of your business home boy, but if you must know I'm her brother, the player that's gone keep you from dating my sister." Click.

The sound I heard as her brother hung up on me. Why he hang up on me? I was just trying to start some friendly conversation. Let me find her cell phone number. That's the number I should have called in the first place. Here it goes.

"Hey, Alicia, I just called your house phone and your brother answered and was very rude. As a matter of fact;" *before I could finish my sentence I was interrupted with,* "this *is* her brother, Negro. Don't call my sister any more Justin. You got to go through me first to get to my sister and from the look of things you're not going anywhere."

Why? Why does stuff like this have to happen to me every time? What have I ever done to anyone? Right before I could finish ranting to myself, I heard Alicia's voice in the back ground barking at her brother to give her the phone. What a sign of relief that is for me. Now she and I will finally be able to talk.

"Hey, Justin, I thought your Mom didn't want us talking. Don't mind my brother; he can be a jerk at times. He's only fourteen and has this deep voice that scares everyone away. Believe me, he's completely harmless. If you see him, you'll know what I'm talking about."

"Oh, ok." That chump, wait till I see him. "That's what my Moms says but my heart doesn't care about all of that." I told Alicia.

"Ok, well I wish I could talk to you more, but

I AM THE SECRET!

I really got to go to work so I'll talk to you some other time." Alicia said, as she rushed me off the phone. And rushing away all the things I had to say to her for that moment.

"Alright, save some shrimp for me."

"I won't, but I'll make sure to save you a kiss the next time you come by."

"Alright, bye!" *Wow, now that's what I'm talking about! The girl really knows what she wants; there ain't no hesitation to her game. I need to talk to older chicks more often. And the good part is, this girl has money. She could take care of me, drive me around town and feed me for free, at my favorite restaurant. It'll be like heaven on earth. Ok, let me snap out of it. Well at least I'll get some free food.*

"Mama!" I yelled out from my room.

"What do you want Boy?" My mother responded.

"I want to talk to you for a minute or two," I met her half way in the hallway.

"Wait a minute, you want to sit down and talk to me. How much money do you want, Justin, and what do you need it for?" She looked confused.

"Mom, I don't want money, I just want to talk to you about some serious stuff," I reassured her with a hug and a kiss.

"You wanting to talk to me? This is like. Like heaven on earth."

"You can say that again. Will you please come sit down with me in the living room?" I pleaded with her once more.

"Ok, Justin, only a few minutes. I have some peas and turkey legs cooking." *My mother seems to always be cooking; Rick will be a lucky man.*

"It won't take long at all." Let me get my game face on.

"Ok, son, go ahead and speak."

"I just wanted to say that these past weeks have been crazy for me and stuff, you're getting married, me meeting Alicia, and above all, God coming to me in my dream."

"I can tell that this has been bothering you Son. What can I do?"

"I just want to know more about God. I mean, when I was a kid you and Dad taught me a little bit, but right now I want to know more about Him. Ever since I started high school everything seems to be going the same way, one circle after the other. It's all been the same circle of school, band, sex, school, band, sex and sometimes parties."

"You've been having sex? Justin, why?" My mother looked at me with the mad eye.

"Come on, Ma, you should already know this. You thought Mr. Randall was lying when he told you he caught me and Tracey in the bathroom with our clothes off."

"But I thought he was lying like those other teachers. I thought he was picking on you to try to get to me as usual."

"Well mom, that's not the point at this moment, besides, everyone's doing it."

"No, it is the point, Justin. STD's don't go away with a wing and a prayer. Many of them will live with you for a lifetime and some will take your life."

"I shouldn't have even mentioned it, Ma." She is not happy at all. *She looks like she could slap the grits and butter out of me and still make room for left over. I shouldn't have told her. I shouldn't have told her. I thought she'd be more cool and understanding but apparently not.*

"Ok Justin, tell me what's your main point then."

Finally, she's ready to listen to me, "my main point is the fact that I want to stop the cycle."

"Well that's good to know as long as it doesn't include you quitting school."

"Ever since that dream I've been feeling pretty weird about myself. It's as if God is starting to reveal everything that's wrong in my life. I can't take the guilty conscience."

"Baby, God will show you as much as you are willing to let him in on your life to see. What's happening to you now is the subtle will to change your life as you know it."

"So what do I do now, what do I say to God, what do I say to anybody?" *I'm confused. Just the other day I was talking about having sex with Alicia, now I'm talking about God changing my life. What is going on with me?*

"Before you say another word, this is what you do. Say this prayer with me: Jesus, come in to my heart, cleanse my soul, come into my mind and make me whole. I am a sinner and you've died for me, so Jesus please Jesus set me free. I believe that you are the son of God and I confess with my heart that I am saved by the blood and death on the cross so you can give me life and life eternally. I acknowledge your Lordship in my life. Have your way in me now and always."

Justin, Baby, by saying that prayer you have now entered God's kingdom. The road will be tough and the temptations tougher, but I believe with God all things are possible. Boy, we are going to church tomorrow. I know you and Precious haven't been in a long time, but tomorrow you'll be able to receive the answers better than I can give."

I don't remember ever crying, at least not in a while, but right now I find myself shedding a few tears. I feel such relief. Is this the future that God has for me, crying and weeping, weeping and crying? If so, I don't think I want that future.

"Let the congregation say Amen!" The pastor shouted out with a Bible slinging around like a baseball bat in his hands. One more swing and we're all out of here.

"Amen," the congregation said in a chorus of voices. *Isn't that something, Alicia goes to this church too? I think I'm really going to like this church.*

"Choir you may be seated. Before I get into the scriptures, I want everyone to picture what I'm about to talk to you about. Today's title is, 'God in my dreams'."

That immediately, sent chills down my spine. I immediately felt a rush of blood surging to my heart as he announced the title. I guess that's just another mysterious way God works.

"Many of you today in the congregation are trying to decipher between a dream from God and a dream from yourself. Here's a hint folks; most of what you dream has some sort of attribute of God, whether directly or indirectly related. Because to look at our very existence in the book of Genesis, we are all created for the purpose of God, and what better purpose besides faith, praise and worship than dreams.

Dreams to me are the seeds in which hope comes from. Ladies and gentlemen, in order to have faith, you must have something to be faithful in. And for fellow believers, that something is God.

Faith is the substance of things hoped for, and the evidence of things unseen. What do you see in the dream or vision which God has placed in your spiritual binoculars?" The pastor looked around at the whole congregation.

"One thing I like about binoculars has to be the unfaltering ability to see at a distance. Although you are a mile away from that thing you are looking at, the binoculars give you the vision to see it as if you were right next to it. That's how your faith has to operate folks. Can I get an Amen?" He requested, with tadpole size drops of spit rushing out of his mouth.

"Amen." Went the church, and, "hallelujah"

said the choir.

"There is no need to be afraid or scared about the dream God gave you. Love it, cherish it, and build upon it. He didn't give it to you for no reason. Remember brothers and sisters, there is a purpose for everything in life, and who are we to judge the purpose God has set forth for ourselves and even each other."

I glance over and see mama boo-hoo crying.

Precious is wiping up her snot while Rick is trying to comfort mama. I don't know why she's crying and right now I don't want to know.

I resumed listening to the pastor, "So right now we're going to open up the doors of the church to all those whom need to get saved, and for the brothers and sisters out there who decided to give up their dreams and feel like it's no longer worth pursuing. Come on choir sing, 'I need you'.

All rise please, as the choir sing: I want you; I want all of you to come who's been hurting, feeling lonely, down and depressed. Now is the time for you to come down and understand that God gave you joy and peace. With joy my brothers and sisters, you can drink. God said you can drink from the well of salvation. Come on somebody! Don't get caught up in the web of doubt and rhetoric, come forward to Jesus and he will give you rest.

Come forward folks, come forward, yes, yes keep coming. All you who felt like giving up, tired of going in circles in your life, feeling like doing the same things is just too much. Why don't you come?"

That is my cue; I'm going up there, to find the answers I've been missing. I've been spending too much time asking Ma about God, than asking God what He feels. How dumb is that?

Now everyone's looking at me clapping, clapping their hands, here comes the break down and now the prayer. This man's breath is a little warm, but, oh well, I'll take it.

"Lord Jesus I pray you cast out the demons from this boy's mind. I pray Lord that you release all things off his life that do not belong. Father, I pray you empty the store houses of heaven and wash this child clean as snow. Create in him a clean heart, a pure mind free from persecution, addictions, impurity, doubt, worry and fear. Lord Jesus give him a new mind, a new will, and a new way to live his life, Lord. Let him live his life for you and you alone. Jesus, Jesus, Jesus! By your strength, your will, and courage I say, Amen."

"Are you saved son?" The pastor whispered in my ears. "Well kind of sort of; Mom told me some things to get saved."

"Who's your mom?" He questioned with a sure authority.

"Ms. Sandra Lewis." I silently said.

"Sandra Lewis? You're Rodney's boy Justin? Little Justin? Wow, it's been a long time since I seen you, Son. Where is your sister Precious?"

"Her and my mom are right down that aisle way," I pointed. Precious and Mama is still blowing snot out of their nose.

"Ok, son, this is what we're going to do. I'm going to have you to repeat the prayer of salvation and pray for you again."

"Ok." *Didn't I just do this the other day. Maybe I'll be over saved, if there is such a thing.*

"You ready? Just repeat after me," he grabbed my hands.

As I repeated after him I felt such a calmness, all the distractions faded away. I even forgot the fact that Alicia was there. The last thing I knew I was getting up from the ground with oil on my head. The pastor said I was baptized in the spirit as we prayed. He had cast out whatever evil was in me, and he even spoke healing over my life for whatever was to come. So much for Mom saying things can't happen with just a wing and a prayer.

This day forward I will walk and talk as a new man. Right now I have a new life waiting for me. For God so loved the world that He gave his only begotten Son, that whosoever believes in him shall have eternal life. Right now I believe. I believe I'm going to heaven and nobody can stop me from getting there.

Just how can I explain all this to Alicia? I'll find some kind of way to dress it up. I guess this means now I can't lie since I chose to go with God. As for premarital sex, well, let's just say that I'm a work in progress. I remember my mama telling Precious and I that fornicators don't make it to heaven. She told us that all the time after Dad had cheated on her. I want to make it to heaven, but I know that the walk is hard, and living this Christian life is even harder. God help me.

I AM THE OLIVE TREE

"How much stronger could you be if your roots are rooted in an olive tree? Class can anyone tell me the significance of olives in our everyday life." The art teacher asked with his back to us.

Here we go again, another weird assignment from our art teacher. Maybe God should enter his dreams and tell him to wake up and smell the coffee.

"I can't believe it. No one would like to share the very purpose of olives in our lives?" *I hope he doesn't call on me, for all I know, people use olives to cook with and throw oil on folks to cast out devils.* "Very well then class; let me start out with a few basics on such a great and magnificent tree. The olive tree is an evergreen tree or what some would like to call a shrub which is usually native to the Mediterranean and Asia.

Although this tree produces some of the smallest fruit, the very nature of the tree can stand against the rest of them. When people generally think of olives; they think of purity, love, peace, and of course for most of you folks, toppings for your salad or oil to cook with.

Yes that is correct, but what makes an olive significant? It is its ability to have a long shelf life. Most fruit die once fallen on the ground. Well olives, let's just say they just tend to carry on a life of their own. Today, I will show you a picture of an olive tree if you have not been fortunate enough to see one for yourself.

The assignment for today is to draw your ideal olive tree. Now mind you class, there is no right or wrong way to do this. On Friday we will all share with the bringing of olives and each one of you will show us exactly what you would do with it.

We have a few minutes left before the bell rings, so I'll pass the picture around to each row."

Five, four, three, two, one goes the bell, off to lunch I go, but first I'll stop by my Mom's class. I guess I'll make My mom feel loved and all, since she's getting married now.

"Hey, Justin- boo, what's going on?" My mother eased my spirit.

I hate when she adds the 'boo' part to my name.
"I'm good Ma, just getting out of my favorite class."

"Let me guess, Art?"

"Yep." I acknowledged with humility.

"So what did you all talk about today?"

"We talked about the olive tree, the teacher was talking about how great and unique it is. We have to draw our version of the olive tree we seen today, and we have to write down what we would do with our olives."

"What does he mean besides eating and cooking with it?"

Here we go. "You know how he can be, wanting us to dig deep and think beyond the surface.

"So have you thought of something?" My mother looked up at me.

"Not really," I told her nonchalantly.

"When is the project due?"

"This Friday." I said with a smile.

"Well you better get to thinking. *You* know how he loves to call you out. Speaking of calling you out, isn't this your lunch hour?" She batted her eyes at me.

"Yeah," I responded with a smirk.

"Well you better get to lunch, Boy. I don't want you to be late for your English class. The last thing I need is the teachers saying that my own son can't show up to my class on time."

"Alright, alright. I won't be late, even if I have to eat the rest of my lunch in here."

"You have about twenty minutes left. Hopefully one of those pretty girls will let you skip the line. I love you, baby. Have fun at lunch."

"Ok Ma, what is twenty minutes going to do for me? I need more time than that," *Why is this hallway congested? Oh no! It's a fight! I'll never make lunch at this rate, but hey a fights a fight, I'll miss my lunch for this. Oh boy, here comes good ole' Principal Adams here to save the world. She's gone get enough of trying to break up fights. The woman is so old; I could break her jaw with my pinky finger. Oh no, Mom is rushing out the door headed to the fight, I have to go save her.* "Mom, what are you doing?" I struggle to pull her back.

"Boy, get your hands off of me. I have to go to the bathroom if you must know," she pulled away from me with her long blue dress and high heels on.

"I thought you were running over to the fight, I was afraid you might get hurt.," I explained.

"I don't have time for fights, not in my heels and long dress. I leave fights to the principal. As far as I'm concerned, the only fight I want to be in right now is a fight to the toilet. So I'll see you in about fifteen minutes. Don't worry; I know it's going to be hard to get lunch now, so I'll give you a pass once you get to class. See you in a few minutes."

"Ok, Ma."

I wonder who was fighting. I can't help but be nosy. I knew it had to be Cece going at it again. That girl loves to fight. She might get expelled this time around. It's always something with that girl. She fought Bria, her longtime rival, both of those chicks will be in the hot seat. Bria has always been getting off easy because her daddy's a lawyer. He loves to cry self defense, and lawsuit against the school. He does have a point because Cece has to be at least two feet taller weighing twenty more pounds than Bria.

Those girls have been fighting each other ever since elementary school. Both of them got kicked out of school at one point, all to arrive at the same high school with that mess. I wonder who started the beef anyway. In a woman's world, fighting is all about the man, jewelry and gossip. I haven't met a female yet that can get along with another female for more than fifteen minutes without getting into some kind of argument. Even my mom and Precious can have their moments; I have to occasionally play mediator for them two.

"Justin, I want you to be back in class in thirty minutes, I don't need you taking any hour long breaks."

"Oh Ma, I'll be back before you pick your head up."

Shoot, Mama shouldn't have given me this pass. I'm going to check out the ladies, find out more about the fight, and, oh yeah, eat. It is so beautiful sometimes to have a Mother who also teaches at the school you attend. Hey, who ever said, it doesn't have its share of rewards? Here comes the assistant principal ready to bother me.

Wow! That's strange, the assistant principal walked right past me. Something's wrong. That man usually runs out of his office just to see what I'm doing out of class. He walked by me like I was his imaginary friend.

"Hey girl, what you doing?" I said to one of the young honey's passing by.

"Minding my own business, Justin. Go to class. What you doing out here anyways?" She rolled her eyes and sucked her teeth back at me.

"Girl I'm bout to eat lunch. Why you stressing me though, like something wrong with me?"

"It ain't that, just trying to help you out, you know you are known for walking the hallways." *She's obviously bringing up the past about me.*

"Well, I got a pass." I flashed it at her with a cocky grin.

"That's because your mother works here. If it wasn't for your mama, you'd be having detentions all day long. Mama's boy!" *Oh, no, she done gone too far!*

"I ain't no Mama's boy, and don't hate because I can get around and you can't. Tell your mama to get her degree and become a teacher."

"I know you ain't talking about my Mama!" She growled back at me.

"Well, don't talk about my mama." *I can tell she's getting mad now. I done pushed her buttons.*

"I'm out of here Justin, you're lame," She quickly deflated her anger.

"Alright, bye." *This girl has wasted ten of my minutes, my mom is going to be pissed if I get to class after thirty minutes; I better hurry up and go to lunch.*

"Glad to see you've made it back on time Justin, right now everyone's doing their journal writing and the topic of discussion is worst life ever. I want you to write in five paragraphs, the worst experience you've ever had."

What the heck does she mean by that? I only have one life to live.

"I know the topic seems strange but it will make perfect sense later."

"Ok." Let's see, worst life ever.

My worst life ever had to have been the time when I found out that my father was sleeping with Ms. Hamburger and a step brother was on the way. His name is Joseph and he's ten years old now. From the time he was three he was talking about ruling the world, talking trash about me bowing down to him and serving him. I hate that kid, he's not a good sport; loves to cry to his Mama and stick his tongue in my face.

Although I don't really like Joseph, he's still my father's son. Looking at Joseph sometimes reminds me of myself. Maybe one day he will grow up to be the king he wishes to be. Anything is possible. Who would of thought that America would have voted for it's first black president in my lifetime?

Yeah, maybe Joseph will be something some day, but he won't be no ruler over me. I don't care if he's voted head of the U.M., I mean U.N. So I guess my worst life ever couldn't be that bad after all. Besides, I still have to speak to the brat.

"Are you finished?" My mother asked me.

"Yep." I told her nonchalantly.

"Let me read it." She stared at me.

"No, it's describing my hate for my step brother Joseph. It might be a conflict of interest."

"If that is how you feel about your worst life ever, then that's your opinion Justin. Don't worry, I'll read it a little later." She reassured me. "Ok, class, times up. Everyone should be finished with their five paragraphs.

In writing about your worst life ever I didn't

want to give you any hints or clues as to why you wrote what you wrote. I wanted all of you to use your imagination and figure it out for yourself. Before I let you all share, I'm going to read mine very quickly."

Is she crazy? I hope it has nothing to do with me. Of course the whole class is looking at me now. I might as well have a knife to my neck for how hard the class is looking at me. I'm ready to leave now; I don't have time for this. I really don't want to be embarrassed. Here she goes.

"My worst life ever was a life I always thought I had, yet I didn't. This little life of mine seemed to make everything out to be perfect, sweet and kind. I thought my husband loved me, I thought my career was advancing, but with the sudden turn of events, it all vanished.

How can I, a grown woman live in such a fantasy world, when the world I live in had changed? When God gave me the right to give birth and the seeds from my womb are waking me up in the morning screaming Mommy. It was not the glory of motherhood and love for my kids that gave me the worst life ever. It was the scars from an ex-husband torn between love and lust for another woman.

I still live with these scars everyday, and if I did not live in such a fantasy and thought to see my husband for who he really was, then what turned out to be my worst life ever, will now be my best life ever. And as of this year, I found a new life in a new love. A love I am grateful to explore and appreciate for what it's worth.

In realizing my worst life I understand that my father in heaven brings out the best life, once we seek and follow him."

Everyone is clapping. *I'm crying, and my Mom is crying too. Only if Precious was here, then we'll all be crying together. I'm surprised that she mentioned God so many times in school, but I'm happy that she let go of what's been on her mind for a while.*

"Class, do you all have your assignments on the olive tree? Good, do I have any volunteers?" *He better not call me, I'm busy.* "Mr. Peterson in the back, would you come forward and be so kind to share with the class what you would do with your olives."

"Well sir, for my presentation." As usual, the art teacher cuts him off.

"To the front of the class Mr. Peterson." *I'm glad I didn't have to go first.* "Uh, Mr. Lewis you will be next after him so be prepared and ready to go. After Mr. Lewis I will have Rebecca," *I shouldn't have spoken so quickly. I wanted to go last, which would have probably meant, I wouldn't have to present today.*

"Hello class, my name is Robert Peterson and I'm about to tell you what I would do with my olive. Here is my lettuce; here is my tomato, a little ranch dressing, ham, and my olives to top it off. So as you can see, my use for olives would be with my salad to keep me healthy. And now I don't have a great, but excellent salad to eat, thanks to the olives from such a great tree."

"Well done, Mr. Peterson." *That's it? My step*

brother Joseph could have thought of that. "Mr. Lewis, are you ready to present, sir?"

"Yes, I am," I lied.

"Well, come on up then. Tell the class what you feel about the use of an olive in your everyday life," He directed me to the front with his index finger.

"Of course everyone should know my name by now, but if you don't, I'm Justin Lewis. I brought some olive oil, my air Jordan's, and a polishing rag. What I'm about to do is pour a little of the oil on the rag, polish up my shoes and there you have it. Now you may ask what makes this so special.

Not only does it save me money on having to pay for shoe polish, but it is environmentally friendly, and when I'm not polishing up my Jordan's, I can cook me a good meal with it."

"Good job, Mr. Lewis. I need a little polishing of the shoes myself. Ms. Rebecca are you ready to present? After Rebecca will be Leroy, then we'll take a little intermission and talk a little more about olive trees. You ready?"

"Yes, I'm ready." Rebecca said hesitantly. "Hello, my name is Rebecca Roberts and what I decided to do was um heat up the olives in the oven at three-hundred and fifty degree temperatures for about ten minutes. Then I took them out and drew this beautiful canvas with the peels of the olives. This whole design is made out of roughly one-thousand olives, all with their peeled skins, kind of gives it like a three dimensional feel."

"Wow, that is very beautiful and unique. I must say, Ms. Rebecca, you've done well. Leroy, you have quite some shoes to fill here and I'm not talking about Jordan's. Are you ready?"

"Yeah, kind of. I really don't have much. Give me a moment." *What the heck does he have in his hands?* "To all of you all who don't know, this is an olive branch; it's often used as a symbol for peace. Many scholars say that it's one of the best ways to make up to a girl. Regardless of what the scholars say, I'd use it for peace because peace is what we need in this country. I actually have a piece of an olive branch with a real olive on it to give each one of you. The best way to stop a fight or I guess try to get the girl, is to just hold up your olive branch and good things will come to you."

"Very good, Mr. Leroy, I am highly impressed with you and all the presenters whom have shared their uses of the olive with the class today. All of you have done a wonderful job. Class, let's give them all a hand. Now for my presentation, then we'll get back to our presentations. Just to give you a heads up, Katrina you will be up next, then Stacey after you.

Olive trees ladies and gentlemen, as you have just seen, have many different uses. They can be used for peace, love, artwork, shining shoes and even salad to name a few. The purpose of this project was to allow you to stretch your mind with something so simple as a little olive. Now we'll have Katrina to present."

I think I should give her my olive branch she is oh so beautiful. She would make a man spill milk all over his clothing. The girl's got a body for days and she knows it, she has to be one of the finest girls in this school. But who am I kidding? I'm talking to Alicia now, and I'm trying to get my life right at the same time. The last thing I need is two chicks fighting over me, then I'll really have to wave the olive branch.

Now that I've done my presentation, I'm actually glad I went. I don't have to worry about being real good or trying to do a better presentation than someone else. Now I could just sit back here and shoot a few text messages to a couple of friends and close associates.

"So what did he think?" My mother asked, looking at me with her hands on her hips.

"What did who think?" I said.

"What did you art teacher think about your presentation?" She asked again.

"Oh he liked it, Ma. The whole class liked it. At first I didn't want to go today. But I'm happy I got it out the way."

"That's good. He's been telling me that you're doing better in his class. He's proud of you too, I just want you to know that."

Wow! Mr. Art teacher actually cares about me; I thought he was joking when he talked to me the other day. Maybe he's not like the other teachers; maybe he really does want to see me become successful.

"Well that's cool. What are we having for dinner?"

"We will be having Salisbury steak with

black olives on the top, cornbread, mash potatoes and broccoli."

"Let me guess, Rick is coming over?"

"No, not tonight. I thought the three of us should have some time alone together before Ricky moves in with his kids."

Oh, ok, that's a surprise; Ricky's been over here every night for dinner. I probably know the amount of hairs coming out of his nose, as much as I've seen him. "Yeah, I would really like for us three to talk and enjoy each other's company. I don't remember the last time the three of us alone had a real conversation. I would really like that, so go ahead and do what you do, and I'll be in here slaving over the food."

"Can I be your master?" I joked with her.

"Boy, get out of here!" My mama gave me the look, as I scrambled out of the room.

I'm glad that moms is in a good mood. I love my Mom, and she's cool when she wants to be. Let me check on lil sis and see what she's doing.

"Precious, what are you doing in my room?"

"These are condoms!" Precious scolded me while shoving them at me. "I thought you said you were going to stop having sex."

"Um, when did I say that?" *She is trying me now.*

"Wasn't that the commitment you made to God when you went up there this past Sunday?"

"Yeah, sort of; But more so it was about getting my life right and better, and to be honest with you, my life was going better till I caught you snooping around in my room. Even mama doesn't go through my stuff like this." *I usually don't get mad at Precious, but this time I'm furious.*

"You'd be surprised at what Mom knows. Justin, just because she doesn't say nothing doesn't mean she doesn't know!"

"Well it doesn't mean that you need to know too. Get out of my room."

"Hey, hey, hey what's going on back there? Justin and Precious, this is supposed to be a quiet and joyful day for us, not a day of arguing and yelling."

"Everything is ok, Mom," I call out. "Yo, look, I'm sorry for yelling at you lil sis; it's just that I don't like people looking all over my stuff. It's an invasion of privacy."

"Ok, ok I get it. I'll never come in your room again."

She's mad now. "You know I still love you though right."

"Yeah, but I don't know what's happening to me, Justin. I'm really beginning to like boys. It feels like some kind of gravitational force is pulling me to them. There's this one guy that's always looking at me and he's sooo cute. What do I say? What do I do? How do I control what I'm feeling about him? Tell me, Justin, tell me." She pleaded.

"Sis, here's the break down. Me, Mom or Nobodyelse can stop you from doing what you want to do, because what you really want to do will end up happening anyway. There is some things I've done, things I've said that I have to suffer the consequences for, because that was the choice I made. Just a few weeks ago I practically hated God and all the principles he stands for, while calling myself a Christian.

It wasn't till God came into my dream, that I realized that I was given a choice, a choice to either do better or do worse. No I'm not saying that either will happen over night, but one of the two will happen over time. Before I had the dream all I could think about is girls, smoking, sex, and a few booze. I would like to say that I don't still think about those things, but I think about them in lesser proportions. Maybe one day all those thoughts and feelings will vanish away. I just got to renew my mind daily lil sis.

My Art teacher had this assignment for us to do on the mighty olive tree. Now talking to you, I can really see what that assignment means. All of us are given the same start in life in terms of like being born. Being born is our roots and the olives are the fruit that's produced. Seeing the many different uses people had for one little olive was amazing!

So I say that to say, with every tree we are given a fruit and its up to us to determine its use in our everyday lives. Me, I decided to use olive oil to shine up my Jordan's."

"No you didn't, that's crazy!" Precious laughed.

"That's what I thought at first, but look at the J's Precious, they still shining."

"But what does all this mean for me and the boy I'm beginning to fall in love with?"

"Girl that ain't nothing but puppy love. What it means to you is that you already have the answer, and the tools to make your life be whatever. I can't stop you from having sex, just like Mom can't make me go to class. Well at least if it ain't her class. You kind of get my point now?"

"Yeah, I do, so will you give me a few condoms?" *She threw me off with that comment. I'm in trouble now.*

"Precious, are you trying to get me killed?"

"I was just kidding. If mom finds out I was even thinking of having sex, I'd get myself killed."

"Precious, just be careful, and if you really feel like you have that urge to do it, just come to me and we'll talk about it. I wouldn't want you to catch nothing and I'm definitely not ready to be Uncle Justin."

I AM THE PROVIDER

"Dear Lord, gracious Holy Father in heaven, Oh benevolent Lord over all the earth. Mighty is your name and wondrous is Your powerful praise." Just say the grace already mom. "We just thank you for such a beautiful time of matrimony." What? "And the breaking of this great bread, feast of lambs and peace that be." Feast of lambs? I thought we were having Salisbury steak. what is she talking about? "We thank you and adore you for this food, Father in Jesus name, we pray, Amen."

Wow. I almost thought she was going to recite the pledge of allegiance with that. She really needs to start being short on her prayers over grace. If I had a tape recorder, I could record her, and write a book on all the silly stuff she says in her prayers over dinner; took her to get to heaven to even mention something about the food.

"Why are you so quiet over there, Justin?" My mother inquired of me.

"I'm just enjoying the food mom." *What I'm*

really doing is trying to hurry up and eat what's left of this food growing cold after her long winded prayer.

"So Precious, how was school today, Baby?"

"School was alright. This one girl got on my nerves and one of my teachers is starting to give me too much homework. Oh, and another thing, the cafeteria food is so disgusting. Mom, you have to give me more money so I can order food with my friends sometimes. Only the geeks and poor people eat in the cafeteria."

"Sister girl when I last looked around, we aren't poor, but we sure aren't rich. It takes a lot of money for you to wear all those labels and brand name clothes. It's hard times for a lot of folks right now, including us. Never look down on your neighbors, Baby, because that can be you one day. The good book says that the first will be last and the last shall be first.

Hey look at me, Precious; my grandmother always told me to be careful how you treat folks because they could surely be as an angel amongst you in disguise."

"I know, mother. I just hate the food, and I don't want to look un-cool in school."

Good, those two are going back and forth now, I can finish eating and chill. Maybe play a little bit of Halo tonight.

"Since when did going to the cafeteria make kids look un-cool, your brother Justin goes there everyday, along with hundreds of his peers."

"Am I excused from the table now?" I asked

with an attitude.

"I'm sorry, Justin. Listen, I wanted to talk to you both about Rick and the wedding. But most importantly, I wanted some feedback on living arrangements after the wedding. I just want to make sure you both are comfortable with Rick and his children moving in."

"Does it matter, mom? You two are getting married. It's not like we could kick the kids out and tell them to live in a tree house outside." I showed my mother my frustration.

"You have a point, Justin, but what can we do to make this a much easier transition for both them and us? Right now we have the office as a room they can use, and possibly one of them can sleep out in the living room. What I was thinking about is getting a bunk bed and put it in one of your rooms since your rooms are bigger than the office room. Which one of you will stay in the office?"

"She will." I told my mom.

"He will." Precious quoted my mother.

"Ok, well let's flip a coin for it. Which one of you wants to pick heads? Heads means you stay, tails means you go."

Wow. The future of my privacy and our rooms is based on twenty-five cents? What is this world coming to? I'm ready to chill.

"I choose heads," I said.

"Here it goes as I throw it up, let it fall on the floor, and Precious tell us what side it landed on."

"Tails. Ha, ha, ha." Precious laughed at me

with pleasure.

"Looks like you have to give up the room, Justin." My mother told me.

"I'm out of here, I'll see ya'll in an hour." I voiced my displeasure.

As if this marriage wasn't already becoming dreadful. Now I have to move out of my room of ten years for some new comers just to meet their accommodations. This ain't the Holiday Inn, if it was up to me I'd have them sleeping on the floor in the living room. Shouldn't I have some seniority around here since I'm the oldest? But no, I fell for some stupid bet. I don't want to move. Let me call Alicia to see if she's working tonight.

"Hey Alicia what's up?" I tried to sound happy instead of feeling sorry for myself.

"Nothing much, I'm just here watching TV."

"What are you doing?" She questioned me.

"Walking around the neighborhood." I responded.

"Why?" She questioned me once more.

"I'm mad at my mom and Precious."

"Siblings, siblings, siblings: tell me about it. But why are you mad at your Mom?" She sounded sincere.

"Because she's the ring leader in all of this." *I guess I'm just mad.*

"Oh, I know that feeling," She took a deep breath.

"Hey, can you pick me up?" *Realizing I need to depend on Alicia, I feel like a little boy.*

"Yeah, I can be there in like thirty minutes. What do you want to do?"

"Anything that gets me in trouble." *I am very serious when I say that.*

"Boy, you better stop playing; we're not at that level yet. Besides, weren't you just in front of the church giving your life to Christ?" *I thought she'd never ask me about that.*

"No that was my twin, I heard all about him."

"Stop playing, boy, you don't have a twin. That was you, and I'm so proud of you," she spoke softly through the phone, giving me chills all through my body.

"For what? All I did was have a pastor's breath down my neck with his dragon breath. He needs to pay his tithes to fresh breath."

"I'm proud of you because you went up there and took the first step. The first step is usually the hardest no matter who you are. I myself struggle a lot with my daily walk with God, many things I can't even tell you about."

"Things like what?" My curiosity has been peaked.

"You know, private things, things that I probably wouldn't even tell my husband when I'm married and seventy three years old."

"Darn girl, it's that bad?" *I think she's a freak.*

"Yeah!" She said with a voice of gloom.

"Well, that's cool if you don't want to talk about it. Just hurry up so we can chill."

"I'll be there in thirty minutes." She told me.

Walking around this neighborhood reminds me of the times daddy used to walk me around telling me I need to dream big dreams, create big goals for myself. I was like four or five then, but he was always telling me that I needed to be a man no matter what age I was. Well Daddy, you was right, because I am the man. I became the man you never were, when you were sleeping around with Ms. Hamburger.

"Hey, you made it." I am so happy to see Alicia.

"Yeah it took forever to figure out how to get here. So, where do you want to go?" Alicia questioned with those perky eyes and soft as a feather cheek bones.

"We can go to the mall and grab a dessert." I smiled at her.

"That sounds good. You know, Justin, I'm technically not supposed to be with you."

"Why? You're not supposed to be with me because you're a few years older than me? Because my Mom disapproves? Alicia, I am tired of people in my life always trying to tell me what to do. The truth of the matter is, I don't care about all that noise that other people talk."

"Well done Mr. Speech maker. It's not really all about that, Justin. I'm just afraid that we could slip up and do something we're not suppose to do. Your Mom could take me to court if she found out."

"We'll be alright, don't worry about her. Besides, my Mom has a marriage to worry about." *I knew this wasn't going to be easy for her, being with me.*

"Let me make this left turn right quick. Look at that knuckle head trying to bully his way in front of me in this traffic." Alicia scolded.

"That guy's face is so red he could probably burn a hole through hell."

"Tell me about it. Yep, there goes the birdie. What an idiot! He can stick his middle finger all the way down to hell! We are almost at the mall anyway." *Wow, I have a feisty one on my hands, I like that.*

"Don't worry about that, girl, I'll treat us to some milk shakes and we'll just chill and walk around the mall."

"You got some money?" Alicia asked while staring me down.

"Of course I got some money, just enough to buy you and me a small milk shake."

"So in other words you're broke," she chuckled.

"If that's how you define broke." *What's up with her talking about me being broke?*

"Sounds like we will be doing some window shopping then, is that ok, Justin?"

"Girl I didn't come here to shop, I came here to talk."

"Window shopping is just looking around Justin, not like you're actually buying anything."

"Oh, I knew that," I try to cover my embarrassment.

"Get that spot right there, that looks like a good one, right where that yellow truck on the left is coming out at."

"Yeah, I see it." Alicia told me in a hurry.

"Good."

"I have a question for you, Justin."

This doesn't sound good. "Yeah what is it? What's up?"

"Do you see me more as a friend Justin? Or do you see me more as a hit it and quit it type of girl in your life at this point?"

I knew it was going to be one of those extreme types of questions, and there truly is no way for me to be able to weasel out of this question. If I say hit it and quit it, then she may kick me out the car. If I just say friend, then my luck at hitting it and quitting it may be diminished. So why don't I just say both.

She's looking back at me with those innocent eyes. "I'm waiting for an answer, Justin."

"Honestly, when I first met you at the Red Lobster I was thinking more along the lines of hitting it and quitting it. As I'm getting to know you better, I would appreciate our friendship as well."

"Why did you take so long to answer?" She looked at me hard.

"I was trying to figure out the best way for it to come out." *Hope I didn't screw it up for the both of us.*

"Well that sounds sweet; Justin. Is that what you tell the girls at your high school too?" *Ok, she is starting to annoy me now.*

"No," *Oh, boy. I can see where this is going. The last thing I need is drama between her and I. We haven't even made it into the mall, as a matter of fact we haven't even finished parking.*

"Ok, I'm happy to hear that. Are you ready for those milkshakes?" She smiled back at me.

"Girl, I've been ready!" *That's a surprise. I thought we'd be arguing about this in the car till we're the last people in the parking lot. I must say, she really looks good. She has on the red dress with black poke-a-dots. Her skin is that of a smooth dark chocolate. Her eyes are just as dark.*

Dating an older woman sure has its perks. I get free rides, and my cool points will triple when people start finding out that she and I are seeing each other. Everybody in the band will be giving me a pat on the back. I haven't felt this special, since I was speaking gibberish as a baby. I have to convince my Mom to get me a car sooner.

"Thanks for the shake, Justin. So, what's been on your mind? What would you like to talk about?"

"Nothing's been on my mind, I'm just a little fed up about all this wedding stuff. Rick's kids are supposed to move in and pretty much change my life forever. The bad part of it all is that I'm the one who has to change rooms and stuff. I like Rick and all; I think he's cool and really loves my Mother, but it's his kids I don't think I'll be able to get along with."

"Did you tell your mother or Rick about this?" Alicia asked me.

"No."

"Why not?"

"I just don't want to add on to the drama we

have right now. Also I've been hoping for the best, as far as Rick's kids are concerned. One thing that really, really, bothers me is the changing of rooms. That part had nothing to do with Rick and his kids, it had everything to do with the flip of a twenty-five cent coin."

"So what do you think should happen Justin?" She looked at me very intensely.

"I know, I just don't want to put a lot of stress and burden on my Mom. You should have seen the way she cried in school. She was emotional about her new found love and her past failures, so she decided to let it all out."

"What?"

"Yep."

"Well I'm sorry to hear that." Alicia said with a humble composure.

"It's nothing to be sorry to hear about, it's just the truth to what happened. My mom is strong; she'll get over all that mess."

"So what is it that you think about God, Justin?" *And that question is just the elephant in the building that I needed.* It's ok, because I'm getting a little better with the God thing.

"I think that God is changing my life. He is amazing. Some things have been happening to me that I couldn't even begin to talk about. God is good and I'm glad he chose me."

"So like, how did you feel when you were up in front of the church on Sunday?"

"I was very nervous, embarrassed, and really

wanted to pass the Pastor a breath mint."

"Ouch, I'm going to tell Pastor Hall on you," she joked.

"You make it sound like you two are buddies."

"Yeah, he's my father." Her look was sharper than a two edged sword. *I could have wet my pants at her confession.*

"Oh wow! I'm sorry about that. I didn't know you were a pastor's kid."

"Well I didn't know his breath was that bad." Alicia stated with an attitude.

"So, does this change your perception about me Justin?"

Now I definitely know she's a freak. Most pastors' kids are. "No, it just makes my perception of you that much better."

"Really," she said slyly.

"Yeah, it does. Maybe you and I can do a little one on one bible study and prayer."

"Justin, just because I'm a pastor's kid, doesn't mean I read the bible all day, or prayer twenty-four seven."

"I know, I first met you at Red Lobster remember?"

"Yes, I remember. Who could forget? All I'm saying is that I don't want you to treat me any differently because of my dad. And don't worry, my dad is totally harmless; he has a big mouth with a loving heart. Once he gets to know you, he'll love you."

"Apparently he already knows me. I guess

when I was a kid my parents used to go to that church. I hardly remember anything."

"Well I'm sure you remember something, when I was a little girl I sang in the children's choir. When the children's choir wasn't singing; I sat in the middle section, five rows behind the first."

"I think that's where my parents used to sit. My dad was a deacon in the church, so he sometimes sat on the left side with the other deacons.

That's been so long ago, Alicia. I really wish I could remember." *I'm really getting tired of talking about this too. For me the past doesn't bring with it good memories.*

"Wow, look at the time, its getting late. You ready to go?"

"Yes and no. As far as going home, no; as far as leaving the mall, that's cool." I said to her as she gave me a look of concern.

"Ok, so what else do you want to do? I have to get up early for a class."

"I don't know, I'm just not ready to go home yet." I repeated.

"How about this, we'll take a walk around the park and then I'll take you home. Sounds like a deal?"

"Yeah, that's straight." *I'm supposed to take charge as the man in this friendship, but I can't, I don't have a car or a pot to piss in. I'm young, blessed, but clearly broke.*

"Where you coming from young lady?"
"I'm just coming from the park, Daddy."

"At ten o'clock at night Alicia?"

"Yeah, the park is open all night, Daddy."

"Well who were you with Alicia?"

"Justin."

"Justin who?"

"Daddy, I'm nineteen, I don't have to tell you who I'm dating. And I definitely don't need you preaching to me tonight, Rev. Hall. It's Justin Lewis if you must know."

"Stay away from that boy!"

"What? Why?"

"He's trouble, and isn't he sixteen. Girl you can go to jail."

"Daddy we're not having sex."

"Stay away from that boy, Alicia." Rev. Hall nearly came out of his seat.

"I want to know why."

"His family is cursed. There is a generational curse on that family and I don't want you inheriting it."

"Why would you say such things?"

"Because it's the truth. The boy got more demons around him than the devil!"

"That's wrong! Well you sure didn't act like you're acting now on Sunday."

"When I'm in church I am ordained to provide food for the saints, wisdom to the elders, healing to the sick, and deliverance to the bound."

"Yeah I get it." Alicia rolled her eyes.

"At home I provide pretty much the same with the exception of you being my daughter and me being your father. Are you in love with this kid? You make it seem so hard to get rid of him. I just don't understand why you decided to hang out with a guy that's about three years younger than you. Does his Mom know about you two?"

"His Mother knows a little about us. I first met Justin, his mom, and her soon to be husband at the Red Lobster. It was quite an odd moment for me." She settled her voice.

"Baby I just want the best for you, and would rather you not date him."

"Can you tell me what their family has done, Daddy?"

"Yeah, two words Alicia, lewd wickedness."

"As much as you want me to, I don't want to just put Justin to the side right now. He's a very good speaker. He's intelligent, and he really, really listens to me. Besides, there is no generational curse that God can't cure. That was your sermon on one Sunday in January in the year 2000."

"You sure do have a good memory baby. Whoever your husband is, he sure will have his hands full."

"Listen, listen I know what's right and wrong and I think he's real cute. I'm not talking about marriage Daddy, just friendship."

"Sounds like shacking to me my lovely daughter."

"Daddy!" Alicia cried out.

"Ok, ok I just don't want to see you get hurt, Alicia. I counseled that boy's Mama and Daddy. In fact his father was a deacon in our church ten years ago. Boy, how the time pass. You were about nine years old then. That's when you were really my little girl. You would always obey what daddy said and love me forever. Now you treat Daddy a little rough round the edges."

"Daddy I will always be your girl, but the fact remains, I'm just not your little girl anymore."

"I know, I know. I'm just in denial. You grew up so fast. God, why can't we all just stay young forever? We will one day. We will when we inherit that great kingdom."

"Where's Mom?"

"She went out to the drug store to pick up her prescription. She should be back real soon."

"Ok."

"You know how your mother intentionally gets lost some times?"

"Got that covered."

"Your brother went with her. You know how your brother gets impatient? They'll be back before we know it. I'm getting tired; I want you to remember what I said ok? I'm going to bed. Don't stay up too late."

"I got class in the morning, but I'll try to wait up for them. Good night."

I AM THE PACEMAKER

"Rick, what's going on with you?"

"I'm ok, Sandra, just surfing the web, honey."

"But we have wedding stuff to go over now."

"I know that, I just wanted to check on some of the latest news going on around the world."

"But Rick, you always do this when it's time for us to go over our wedding stuff. I am so sick of this," Sandra complained.

There they go again, arguing. Mom and Dad rarely argued. I am sick and tired of it myself. Let me pull my ipod out so I can get their aggravating voices out my ear. Ok, where is the ipod? Don't tell me Precious took my ipod again. That girl is going to learn to stop touching peoples' stuff.

"Precious? Precious, where is my ipod?" I yell out for her.

"I don't have your ipod, Justin, and why are you calling my name so loud? Maybe you should look under your bed where you keep it sometimes," she yelled back.

"If it's not under there, I'm telling Mama about you always wanting to touch my stuff."

"Tell Mama, I don't care. I will tell her how late you got here the other night." Precious snapped at me.

"So," I didn't give her an ounce of satisfaction.

"Just look under your bed, you know, it's probably there."

"Ok." *I hope it is.*

"Well, what do you see?"

"I found it!" *She's so lucky.*

"Look, you wanted to blame me for your misery as usual. Why did you need that stupid thing so bad anyway?" She stood at my door.

"Because Mom and Dad, I mean mom and Rick, are back arguing again. I hope this is not how it's going to be for the next two years I'm home. If so, I'm moving in with Alicia."

"Ha, ha, ha; yeah right boy, over your dead body. Do you even know who her daddy is?"

"Yes, I do know, he's Pastor Hall."

"I don't know any Pastor that lets his kids have their boyfriend staying nights."

"Well, he may be different. I'm going to tell the pastor that the bible says to be fruitful and multiply." *Let's see what Precious has to say now.*

"Justin you're only sixteen, with what money can you afford to be fruitful and multiply with? You just aren't making any sense. I'm going to get back to doing kids stuff, while you can keep dreaming and fantasizing about Alicia. Besides, that's for married people."

"That's not true, I only dream about what I can't have. Right now she's all mine."

"Don't get your hopes up." She taunted me.

"What did you say?" I narrowed my eyes in warning.

"Don't get your hopes up!" She stuck out her tongue.

"Children, dinner is ready," my mother interrupted us with a shout, bringing us back to reality.

"You better be lucky mom saved your butt Precious."

"Why?" She snorted.

"I was just about to kick it."

"Shut up!"

"You better run," I hopped off my bed, sending her into flight down the hall.

I love my little sister, though sometimes she can drive me crazy. Looking at her makes me kind of feel guilty when I treat girls wrong. Of course I don't tell the girl that, but by Precious being my sister I kind of get like a guilty conscience. I also feel like this though; there is nothing wrong with treating girls wrong, just as long as you know how to treat them right.

Sometimes a relationship needs a little argument and stuff, so the good times could feel even better. Alicia seems too nice to want to argue all the time, but I bet I'll find something, and when I do, well I don't want to talk about that.

"Rick and I are trying to make some final

plans for our upcoming wedding." *If I hear one more thing about this wedding, I'm going to shoot myself.* "So we would just like for you two to say yes you like what we present or no you don't like what's presented."

What's hard about I don't want to participate? I already told my mom before that I could care less about this wedding. Yet, she consistently tries to pressure me to participate. "Ok, Ma, you go ahead and get started." I interrupted her.

"Don't get smart with me, Justin. I'll slap you in front of company and won't think twice about it. Ever since you've been seeing this Alicia girl, you've been really getting the big head. I will straighten your butt in a minute. I know what I need to do, I need to go down to her house and teach her folks a lesson. Who are her parents anyway?"

"Now that's' a little complicated." *If Precious knows, how come Ma doesn't know?*

"No it's not, oh no the heck it's not. Who's her parents Justin?"

"Hey, Sandra, calm down baby, it's alright. Lets talk about that later, and focus on the wedding now." *Rick saved me from my mother's wrath.*

"Look, Rick, don't tell me how to raise my son. I don't tell you how to raise your children."

"I wasn't telling you how to raise Justin, Sandra. In two years the boy will be eighteen. All I'm saying is we really don't need any unnecessary pressure right now. Let's just take all of this at face value and be the good family we ought to be."

"Who are her parents Justin?" my mother ignored Rick's advice. "Answer me now or you're out the band and grounded for the rest of the year." She looked at me with eyes of a wolf, ready to devour me with her words.

Why couldn't she just listen to Rick, and why she got to always threaten to kick me out the band every time I do something bad? It almost makes me not like being in the band anymore. Where is God when you need him? "Pastor Hall is her father Mom."

"What? You mean to tell me the Pastor that's doing our wedding is keeping a secret about his nineteen year old daughter wanting to date my sixteen year old son? Now that's just brutally wrong. Rick we will find us another Pastor as of tomorrow. And as for you, Justin, you're still grounded. You're grounded for a week and you are not to call or see Alicia again. Give me that cell phone."

She is really taking things out of proportion. I don't know what's wrong with Mom. Ever since this wedding junk, she's been acting real different lately. Where is the love, where is the joy, oh, Lord, where is the peace?

"And no son, there is nothing wrong with me, I'm just tired of grown women taking advantage of little boys. We have enough teachers doing that. I am just through; I am so outdone with this mess. As a matter of fact, Rick, call up the pastor."

"Alright, what's the number?"

"Don't you know the number to the church?" She yelled at Rick.

"That's not my church, Sandra. You need to calm down, Baby." Rick tried to console her, but there was no consoling my mother at this point. She has found a cause, and there is no stopping her. She is a woman on a mission.

I AM THAT I AM

*"Class who can tell me the significance between art
and science? Casey, you may speak."*

"Well I think the difference between art and
science is like art is something that expands on
the creativity and science deals mostly with hypothesis."

"Wrong, wrong, wrong; there is no difference."

*Not another day with this teacher. He's coo coo
for Cocoa Puffs. What does he mean there is no
difference between the two? If that was the case, there
wouldn't be a difference between the two classes. This
guy be acting brand new sometimes with his theories. I
bet he calls on me.*

"Mr. Lewis, do you have anything to add to
the conversation? You look rather puzzled back
there."

"No sir, nothing to add." Just like I thought,
he called on me.

"There is no difference class, because just as
science is built upon hypothesis, so is art. If you remember a previous class, we had Justin to tell us his

dream, and each one of you was told to depict what you received from what he shared. Not one of you, I mean not one of you brought in the same drawing. Each one of you brought in something unique, even though he stood up here and told you his actual dream in full length and detail.

So can we conclude that although someone can be in your face telling you something, that you can still misinterpret what they said to you? Mr. Lewis what do you think?"

"You're right" *And right now I'm also thinking about ditching this class.*

"Ditching this class Mr. Lewis would not be the right alternative. The right alternative would be to talk to me after class so we can figure this thing out together. Ok, class, back to the difference between art and science, which I clearly stated that there is no difference."

That's weird, how did he know I was thinking about ditching the class? He had already turned around and looked away from me.

"You see class, art in its very infinite existence can be anything that you want it to be, both created and not yet created. This earth is constantly transforming every day, and every day new life forms are being found, new things are being discovered. What science once said could not happen such as the earth being round, people going out of space or even technology that reads your fingerprints like a highly trained sheriff has happened! So I ask you all once more, what's the difference?

Art is simply the spoken words or imaginative mind that decides to influence the world in a way they see it. Science does the same thing. With just a word God spoke this world into existence and with a word he can speak it out of existence. Just like an artist can sketch a drawing in pencil and then decide he doesn't like it, so then he erases it. So to is the ability of God and all you who are gutsy enough to take the step in creativity.

Can anyone tell me the difference between a tree grown in the desert and a tree grown in the rain forest? Hannah you've raised your hand; what's the difference?"

"One tree needs more water than the other to survive." *That was easy.*

"Hannah have you ever been out to the desert or even the rain forest?"

"No." She looked nonchalantly.

"Well how then do you know what one tree needs and the other tree doesn't?"

"Because that's what I've seen on TV. And that's what I've been taught by my teachers." Hannah shows signs of irritation now.

"But Hannah you have never been to any of these places before, but you know they exist based upon what you heard and what you said you saw. So what if I were to tell you that all that you have heard and seen is a lie, would you believe me?"

"No."

"Why not?" He said with a grim grin.

"Because I know what I saw on TV and what

my teachers told me."

"But Hannah my girl, I've been to the rain forest and I've been to the desert. What are your credentials? You haven't gone to either place."

"Listen sir, I know what I know because that's what my teachers taught me and that's what I read in books and saw on the Discovery Channel."

I hope Hannah doesn't cry now, she's definitely a crier. What is all this craziness about any ways? We are only in art class.

"Now you add that you've read it in a book Ms. Hannah, but how can you believe a book. Where are the facts? Who wrote it? When did they write it?"

"I don't know sir, I don't know; can I go to the bathroom?" *Yep, she's about to cry.*

"Sure, I already have a pass waiting for you with your name on it. Take as much time as you need." He looks disappointed.

"Thanks." Hannah soberly smiles at the teacher.

Maybe this might be my exit strategy, no need to sit around here listening to this crap.

"Class, class your attention please. We have ten minutes left till the bell rings, but here is my point. Just because you haven't been to a place, doesn't mean it does not exist. Just because you see something on television doesn't mean that's what it truly is. The value and heart of the things in this world is astounding.

Art is the matter of things which does more

than meet the eye. You can't just read a book and say oh that's just what it is. You must read to get an understanding, you must study each word to better gain the knowledge and fullness on what the author was saying. Once you learn how to read a book for understanding and truth, you will ultimately learn much more about the author than you think.

Listen here, class. To have a creative opinion is to have an artistic soul which speaks volumes to those whom read, see or speak about your work. Art, ladies and gentlemen is as much science as anything else. Everyday we live art, and when death comes to you, art will continue to spring. Because although the science of a man's body decomposes and withers to dirt, the decomposition of his body provides nourishment and life to thousands of bugs, while at the same time giving back life to all things that grows around it. It's a recycling process ladies and gentlemen, what can be better than that? Class is dismissed, you have no homework tonight. Be prepared for part two in our little discussion on art and science. Mr. Lewis, please come and see me."

I wish he had forgotten. This dude is crazy, talking about body's decomposing being beautiful. I don't know what his Mama fed him for breakfast when he was little, but the dude's got a problem.

"Mr. Lewis, I see that you don't like my class. Is there something wrong, or is there something needing to be discussed?" He looked at me awkwardly.

"There is not much wrong with your class except for you always picking on me and calling me out. Also, I think the decomposing thing was pretty out there too. Other than that man, the class seems to be cool." *Yeah right, this class is worst than a bad game.*

"Are you telling the truth about this class Mr. Lewis?"

"Yes sir, why wouldn't I be telling the truth?" *Ok this dude is scaring me now.*

"Do you know who I am, Mr. Lewis?" *That's obvious. What's his point?*

"Yeah, you're my art teacher." *I responded to his ludicrous question.*

"True, but not good enough. Mr. Lewis, let me make an assertion here. Not only am I you art teacher, but I'm your counselor, your lawyer, your provider, your peace maker, your way maker, your miracle, and most importantly your friend." *He definitely has crazy written next to his name in the dictionary. I never in my life heard such gibberish coming out of the mouth of one man.*

"What are you talking about, sir? You're just an art teacher."

"I know that's what you see me as, but most people see me as more."

"I don't know what you're talking about and what do you mean my, my miracle?"

"Isn't it a miracle that you're in my class Mr. Lewis? Isn't it a miracle that your mother is getting married after years of loneliness and confusion? Everyday presents a miracle Justin; you just have to take the time to see them." *I need a miracle right now, and that is to disappear from this man's presence. He's really starting to creep me out.*

"How did you know about my mother?"

"Because I know that I know. Obviously you weren't just born from the sky or were you? There was only one birth of a virgin and the world knows who that is. In the meantime, Justin Lewis, I must be about my fathers business. I'll see you in class on next week."

As stated before, this art teacher has weird written all across his face and at the same time he's starting to freak me out. I wonder if my mom is putting him up to scaring me, since she finds it difficult for me to date Alicia and keep up with my grades. Whatever he claims to be, I know he's not God. I'll bet my rocked out t-shirt on that.

God doesn't teach art classes and scare high school teens about death. God is some where up in the heavens watching over me. God is too great to come down to this stinking place we call Earth, and why would God want to teach us young sex driven high school kids about art anyways. Like I said, the art teacher is crazy, who ever he claims to be, he should be claiming a nut house.

I wonder what kind of business his father owns; maybe I could get me a job.

"Ma, the art teacher is starting to weird me out."

"Why do you say that son?" She grasped my attention.

"I don't know; maybe because of the way he knows that you and Dad got divorced, and he seems to know what happened in great detail."

"Son, everyone knows that your Dad and I got divorced and I'm sure they know quite a bit of details as well." *Ok this is not working.* "Is there anything else you would like to say Justin?"

"Yeah, he seems to know a lot of stuff that no one else knows."

"That's how he's been for the last one or two years I've known him. He seems to be one of those solitary type of guys. I never ever see him with anyone else. Every once in a while I may glance him praying in the lunch room, but that's pretty much the only time I hear him speak, besides the occasional hi and bye in the hallway."

"He's an alien," said Precious.

"Oh, be quiet girl. Your grounded brother and I are here trying to have a conversation. You haven't spoken to that Alicia girl lately have you, Justin?"

"Nope." *Of course I told a lie. I can't just break away from a good thing that easy. Mama is tripping.*

"Well, I spoke to the pastor and he agreed that you two should not be seeing or talking to each other at least till you turn eighteen."

"Eighteen? She will have moved on, gotten married, and had two kids by the time I turn eighteen."

"Well, that's exactly what the good Reverend is hoping would happen."

"Oh, so you two are plotting against us? I'm

out of here." I turned to leave.

"You wait right there Justin; if you go out that door, don't try to come back to this house." My mother put up a rage.

"Who said I'm trying? Besides Ma, ever since all this marriage stuff you've been acting different. It's time for me to live my life now. Have fun with your wedding."

"Justin! Justin! you get back here." She yelled out at me, at the top of her lungs.

"Bye." I slammed the door on the past.

"That boy is losing his mind. Maybe he's right. Maybe this wedding stuff *is* driving me mad and overboard. Maybe I just need to call Rick, tell him how I feel. I don't know Lord; I don't know what to do." My mother prayed aloud.

"Mommy, who are you talking to?" Precious looked concerned.

"Nobody but myself, Baby. Nobody but myself. Hey Precious, do you think I've changed since the wedding plans?"

"Uh huh. You've been changing a lot Mama. I mean, I kind of understand why, but it seems like you continue to push Justin away. You seem to be getting stricter on us," Precious confessed.

"I'm your Mama. I supposed to be strict." Sandra eyed her pointedly.

"I know that, but Justin is going to be Justin and he really likes Alicia. He's already losing his room, feels like he's losing you, he's lost dad, and now he's losing Alicia." Precious said compassionately, with a tear or two trickling down her face.

"Wow, honey I never thought of it like that."

"Yeah, I know. With all your planning, I kind of understand."

"Maybe I need to just give Justin some space," My mother reasoned.

"I don't really think he's asking for space. Looks like he's asking for his freedom."

"Until he turns eighteen, he's still my responsibility. So, what can I improve on with you?"

"Well, you may not want to hear this."

"Why not? I promise I won't kill you Precious." My mother said with a ghostly stare.

"I... I would like to start dating boys," Precious spoke quickly, shutting her eyes, waiting for the explosion.

"You're right, absolutely right; I didn't want to know. But you know what? I'm not going to say no," She surprised herself with that statement.

"What? Are you serious?" Precious mouth hung wide open.

"Yes. You can date as long as whoever you are dating is willing to come to our house when I'm home. He has to be willing to come by my class room once a week, he has to be saved, and must submit himself to a lie detector once a week. Then and only then will you be able to date. Think you know of someone who can handle that?"

"No." Precious said bluntly.

"Well, then if I find out that you are dating behind my back, then you must submit yourself to a pregnancy test once a month."

"Mom, but that's---."

"It's either this, or wait till you're eighteen to date."

"Six years doesn't sound so bad anymore."

"You're excused."

"Have you all studied the parallels between art and science?" *Another day with the art teacher is all I need to start my life out right. Well, not exactly.*

"Well, my Mama said that what you're talking about is a bunch of crap. She wondered whose strings are you trying to pull?" That was Malcolm speaking up for us all. About time someone told that nutcase that we live in the real world. I mean he's a decent teacher and all, but he's got some issues.

"Well, perhaps I'm pulling your strings Mr. Malcolm. Would you be so kind as to come up here to the front of the class? Now I must tell you, I'm going to ask you a series of questions which you could be right or wrong on. Are you ready for the challenge?"

"Yeah, whatever," Malcolm walked upfront shrugging his shoulders.

"Ok then, first question: What were to happen if I dropped the pen?"

Malcolm has that big smirk on his face. "The pen would fly through the air."

"Good. What happens when sound loses control?"

"I don't know; makes people go deaf?"

"Good."

"Sir, what are you trying to accomplish with these questions?" Malcolm twitched his eyes.

"You've already accomplished it; you may take your seat. Listen class; if you do believe that there is no parallel between art and science would you please stand." That's easy; the whole class is going to stand.

"Anybody?"

I can't believe it. No one stood up. They have to be scared of this man. If they won't stand then I will.

"Mr. Lewis, congratulations. You decided to stand up against me. Now, what is it that makes you feel indifferent from all your other classmates here?"

Now I feel dumb. I shouldn't have stood up. "Nothing makes me feel indifferent. I just don't believe in all this art and science stuff that you've been trying to preach to us. This is an Art class for Christ's sake, not Science."

"For Christ's sake indeed, Mr. Lewis, and please do remember not to take the Lord's name in vain. You may now be seated. Ladies and gentlemen he's right. I shouldn't be mixing Art and Science together in Art class.

Maybe I should just be teaching you all how to draw a beautiful canvas or a clear blue sky so bright that the heavens agree. Maybe I should be up here drawing a few pieces for you. Or maybe, just maybe, all of you young adults will open up your eyes to see the many wonders which Science brings to Art.

Today's assignment is to pick up a flower either from your back yard or grocery store and bring it here, so I could truly show you what I'm saying. Class is dismissed."

Should I go up to him or should I stay in my seat? Decisions, decisions. This teacher is going to drive me crazy. Oh well, I got my Mom's class to attend next. I'm out.

I AM THE
HEALER

"Dad, what are you doing here?" What in the world is going on around here?

"Your Mama called me son, and she told me to come down to see you. Her and I had a great conversation, she told me about the marriage and how she misses me," my father spoke in a tone of fear and regret.

"You left us, and I haven't seen your cheating dead-beat self in ten years. What gives you the right to come around now?" *I couldn't believe my Mom had involved him in our disputes.*

"God, gives me the right Justin. You are *still* my son, and I will always be you father."

He's making me mad now. "Don't come around here preaching, to me. I looked up to you. Man. I thought you couldn't do *any* wrong. You were my Superman, I just about worshipped you." *I had to be screwed up in the head as a kid to worship him.*

"Jesus, is my Superman Justin. Jesus is the

only perfect man to ever walk this earth. We all have skeletons in our closets, Son. Some just seem to be bigger than others. I know that I was wrong, but a little forgiveness would help."

Now he wants to preach to me. Is he crazy? Forgive him? After all we've gone through? "Forgive you for what? Making it tougher for us? Having mom crying at two, three and four o'clock in the morning?" I was yelling at this point, unable to hold back any longer.

"I heard your Mom is getting married. I'm happy for her." *You better be.* "Don't try to change the subject; what are you doing here?"

"Your Mother felt the need for me to see you. She wanted you and I to settle our differences," my father tried to explain.

"These differences don't just settle in a day, they take a lifetime," I reminded him.

"However long it takes, Son, I'm willing to work it out."

"Quit calling me Son; I'm not a little kid anymore," I ranted.

"In my eyes, you'll always be my little Son, but if that's how you feel, I'll just call you by your birth name."

Now he wants to get funny? "So, what time you leaving today?"

"I'm not leaving son, I mean, Justin. I'm here to stay till we work this thing out, even if it takes all year."

"We're good then, you can leave now," I laugh

in disbelief. *Whose coat tail does he think he's pulling?*

"Well, if we're good, then come give your Daddy a hug."

"No." *Now he's trying me, I really need to leave this house. It's either him or me, one of us have to leave.*

"Can't do it, huh, I didn't think you could," he smiled at me with pleasure.

"No, it's not that; it's just the fact that I don't believe in being fake. Kind of like how you were being fake with Mom, having her think you were being faithful," *I aimed for the heart this time. I'm putting everything out there on the table.*

"Son, I thought we've had this conversation already. You act like this is the first time you've seen me in ten years. Now I know it's been that amount of time since I've been to the house, but I I've come by the school a few times. What more do you want from me? I've already apologized. I live with my mistakes everyday. Please don't send me to hell.

All I ask, Son, is for your forgiveness. I know as well as the whole church knows what I have done. Does forgiveness have to be this way? What else do you want me to do?"

Some things are just not right. Here I am wanting to be mad at this joker, but I end up crying. He's over there crying too. I can't stand myself right now. "So Dad, where do we begin?"

"We begin right here, Son. We begin right here. All that is lost is lost and all that is forgotten will be forgotten. But love? Love has a crazy way of healing us all. If God did not love us all he wouldn't

MICHAEL D BECKFORD

have sacrificed Jesus, or saved Noah and his family in the great flood. I know that you're only sixteen now and going through plenty, and a whole bunch of crazy stuff, but listen to me real good: When love enters the picture, the outcome of everything can change.

Your Mother called me out the blue, I was shocked when she told me to come by the house to talk to you. But you know what, Justin? She decided to settle our differences because of the love she has for you.

Right now I just want you to look at this as a healing process taking place between our family. Healing does not always happen instantaneously. Many times it's a residual process that works itself to completely transform and strengthen your life."

Ok, now he's talking a little bit too much. I'm ready to call up Alicia. "So, Justin do you forgive me?"

"Yes I do; I forgive you dad." This forgiveness thing is hard, and it's definitely something that the both of us will have to work out. I'm really not sure what it all means, but if this is what it takes to move on, then I'll take it.

"Now come and give me a hug, son." He quickly grabbed me by the shoulders. *He insists on me hugging him? Oh well. If this is what I got to do to get out of here then I might as well do it.*

"That's my boy. I love you so much, Justin. I love you so much. I'm sorry for all I've done that may have offended you and hurt your mom and Pre-

124

I AM THE SECRET!

cious. I love you son."

"I love you too, Dad, but right now I can't breathe," I managed to get out.

"Oh, I'm sorry. When your Mom gets back I'll tell her that we made up and I can go home now." *Yes! Freedom once more for me.*

"Dad, how far is home?"

"Two hours away." He said.

"Were you really going to stay here for a year?" I pierced my curiosity.

"If I needed to, but now the mission has been accomplished, and I believe that that there is healing in forgiveness."

Ok now it's time for me to rap up this crying session. "Well dad I got some places to be so I will talk to you later."

"Son, it has been a pleasure, take care of Precious and Sandra. Continue to do well in school and just be careful about who you're dating," he warned.

"Mom, told you about that?" *He sounds like he knows something.*

"She just told me bits and pieces of it. Not much for me to say yes or no to. You're right about what you said earlier. You are your own man and you have a lot to look forward to. Just be careful when it comes to beauty, because it may come with a crooked past."

He would be the one to know. "Ok, dad I have to go."

"Ok son remember what I said, healing is in forgiveness. Just like the bible says; if we confess our sins, God will be faithful and just to forgive us of our sins."

I AM THE DELIVERER

"Oh, my God I can't believe it! I'm getting married again!" Sandra said to Lucille.

"Sandra, look on the bright side girl, you get you a new man and a new life."

"But I don't think I'm ready anymore," Sandra sighed.

"Girl, don't get cold feet on me. You have less than two hours till you say I do to Rick."

"But I don't. Justin's father was here last week, talking to Justin about life, and I had a chance to speak to him myself," Sandra confessed.

"And?" Lucille questioned her.

"He's changed; he surely has changed my friend."

"Girl, let me get your mother. You are in love with Rick." Lucille looks at Sandra with complete surprise.

"But I never lost my love for Rodney. I can't be in love with two men at the same time," Sandra groaned.

"Yes, you can! I love my hubby and I love my father too."

"Girl, you know what I mean," Sandra rolled her eyes.

"So, what the heck did you and Rodney talk about that got you all fired up over him?"

"It's not just what we talked about; it's what we didn't talk about that made the difference. The way he looked at me with such humble and meek eyes. The way he blushed about certain moments of our relationship, his total character seemed to be that of a total transformation that only God could do. You know what I mean?" Sandra pleaded with Lucille.

"You sound sold on your Ex, Sandra, you sound sold. So what are you going to tell Rick, the Pastor and everyone else?"

"I don't know. I'm just confused. I am so confused." She continues to plead her case.

"Have you prayed about this?" Lucille asked with ease.

"Yeah, and I believe that God my Father is leading me to go back to the man that fathered my kids. Life is all about forgiveness and reconciliation."

"So what if he cheats again? I thought that he remarried?"

"He's not married, but he tells everybody that he's married. He told me that he tells everyone that he's married because he has always believed that the two of us will be together again. I guess he's right after all.

If he cheats again, then girl, him and I will have it out. But if there is anything I've learned in these past ten years is the simple fact that there are no guarantees in life. Who knows if Rick will end up cheating on me too? Only God knows, only God knows. One thing I *do* know, is the fact that the only guarantee in life is salvation through Jesus Christ."

"Then what are you waiting for Sandra? Call Rodney up, tell him how you feel. Hey, he only lives two hours away. That's enough time for the both of you to say I do. No need in wasting this moment. Believe me he'll be here. Just one more question before you get on the phone. What all did he say to make you change your mind in such a drastic way?" Lucille stared Sandra in the eyes.

"Like I said before it's not what he said, it's what he didn't say. Also, I've heard so many good things about him from outside sources. He's always taken care of the kids, even coming by the school to check on them. I know this seems crazy, but through all the hurt, pain and frustration I went through with him, this time I feel that he's true and ready to spend his life with me and me only."

"Well, look at the bright side, you two are still very young. You're only forty-two and he's forty. Go ahead and call him. I'll pick up and handle everyone else, but you know you have to talk to Rick."

Sandra's voice quenched with fear. "I think

that will be the hardest part."

"I know, I can only imagine," Lucille comforted her.

"Hey, Sandra how are you? Today is your big day. I would like to congratulate you and Rick on your marriage and I wish you two all the success," Rodney said with cheer.

"Well, that's just it Rodney," Sandra hesitated.

"What?" Rodney shouted.

"I need to talk to you about Rick and I," Sandra began to lay the foundation.

"What's wrong? What happened?" Rodney's nerves began to overtake him.

"Well I decided not to marry him anymore." Her voice stood still over the phone.

"Really, wow!" Rodney couldn't believe it.

"Yep, I kind of have conflicting views about the whole thing and I just kind of changed my mind about him." She lightened up a little.

"But you've been dating him for about two years and the other day you were telling me how madly in love you were with him," Rodney reminded her.

"I know, but things have changed. Rick is a good guy and all, don't get me wrong, but things have just changed for me these past couple of weeks. Remember when you and I were talking last week?"

"Yeah." Rodney answered with fear and trembling.

"Well, it was something about you Rodney. When you presented yourself towards me, I guess something about your presence encouraged me to shift directions towards you. I can't believe I'm telling you this, but I want to get remarried."

"What? What a shocker! I wouldn't have ever seen this day coming," Rodney's voice shook with emotion.

"Yeah, that's what my girlfriend said too."

"I'm in total shock." Rodney explained once more.

"So, Rodney would you re-marry me?"

"Yes, yes, yes of course I would, Sandra. I have always loved you and will always love you."

"Well you got an hour and a half left to get here and say I do. Don't worry about a tuxedo as long as you wear a black suit. The colors are red and black. I know that you have plenty of questions, but get dressed and drive down now and ask questions later," Sandra giggled like a young girl.

"Ok," Rodney replied like a soldier called for battle.

"Mommy, who were you on the phone with?" Precious wanted to know.

"Your Dad Miss Nosy," Sandra chuckled.

"Why were you on the phone with him? You're getting married to Rick."

"Well fortunately things have changed."

"What things have changed?" I interrupted Precious and Mom's conversation.

"Oh, even better! I have the both of you to tell

at once. Justin, close the door for me right quick, baby," She shuffled me inside.

"Alright, but what things have changed?"

"Be patient like your sister. I'm 'bout to tell you now. I've changed my mind about marrying Rick."

Well, that's good; now I don't have to leave my room and deal with his kids. Life just keeps getting better for me. Now I get to spend some real good times with Alicia. "Why did you decide to quit Rick?"

"I decided to quit Rick because I decided to give your Dad another chance."

"Yeah, right. You must be joking. Mom, in about an hour and twenty minutes you'll be up there kissing Rick and stuff. Stop playing games with me and Precious. I know you're not serious, especially after all the stuff he put us through." *She has to be kidding. Mom would never do such a thing.*

"I'm serious as a heart beat, Justin."

She is serious. "Have you told Rick yet?"

"I was about to tell him when you two walked in."

"Yes, I get my Daddy back! He's going to be back to protect me, and give me back rubs like he use to. I can't wait to show him that I can make pancakes now," Precious beamed in anticipation.

"Precious, don't get all excited about Daddy, he may go off and leave us for some other woman like he did before, maybe even Ms. Hamburger. Have you thought about that Mom?" I asked, truly disappointed in my Mom's decision.

"Yes, I have, and don't talk to me like I'm your sister. I've thought about it long and hard for the past few weeks. Didn't your father talk to you about forgiveness the last time he was here?"

"Yeah, but I thought you forgave him and moved on. What if he cheats on you again?" I reminded her once more.

"Listen, Justin. There is absolutely no guarantee that he or Rick wouldn't cheat on me, none whatsoever. I have to live my life regardless, and let God handle the rest of the pieces. Yes I've been broken, yes I've been embarrassed, but you know what? A change has come. Your father cheating on me did not make me weak, but essentially a stronger person. You may not have seen it, but by grace I see it now.

Now when somebody throws a left hook, I'm throwing a right. I myself don't completely understand why I'm going back to your father but I know one thing, I love him, and he cares about us."

"What's going on in here? It's about thirty minutes till the wedding starts. I got a little worried that you weren't here. A lot of people in the church were talking about the wedding being cancelled." Rick came in talking frantically.

"You're not supposed to sneak in on the bride, Rick. Don't you know that's bad luck?"

"Oh, my bad. Let me get out of here," he laughed nervously.

"Wait, Rick."

I hate to see the look on his face after she tells

him this. I really feel bad for the dude now because he seemed to be pretty cool.

"What?" Rick responded.

My mother looked down and said, "Well, the wedding *is* cancelled."

"What? What did I do, how come? Can't we talk about this," Rick was in shock.

"It's too late," My mother said, as tears began to roll down her face.

"Why, you didn't even give me a chance. I got all my parents and friends waiting to see me marry you."

"It's not you at all, Rick. It's about Rodney, and I feel that he's the man I need to marry this day."

"But the guy is a loser, you said it yourself! He cheated on you, embarrassed you, and left you alone with the kids!" Rick was more than upset, he was irate.

"I know, I know, but he's also a good father and a changed man of God. I don't know what all happened, but I believed that God has delivered him from his cheating past so he can be a better man for our future. Everyone deserves a second chance, Rick, and he's the father of my kids. Justin really needs a lot of help, Precious loves her daddy and I love him too."

"This is wrong, Sandra, completely wrong. How could you? How could you leave me for your Ex on our wedding day? I am embarrassed, I'm out of here."

"Maybe you and your Ex should try to reconcile your differences, because you also have loving kids to raise," My mother reasoned.

"Me and my Ex Sandra? Come on. Not in a million years. I don't love her, I love you."

"I said the same thing about Rodney; not in a million years, but God has a powerful way of changing people and situations around."

"I'm done!" Rick stormed out of the room.

I know he's hurt, I can't help but feel the hurt rolling off Rick in waves. I hope he doesn't do something stupid or crazy.

"So ma, when will dad get here?" I asked her.

"He should be here in ten minutes. You two do me a favor. Precious, get ready to be my flower girl. Justin, you go up to Pastor Hall and tell him to white out Rick's name and write Rodney's name. Lord, this will be a night to remember. In the meantime, I have ten minutes to finish putting on my pearls and make up. Both of you make it quick."

I hate this, 'Here comes the Bride' song. Sounds like some kind of song that was birthed from a Nursery Rhyme. Well, who cares? My mom looks gorgeous, she looks so happy and I'm happy for that. Everyone is standing up clapping for her. To think that Precious and I weren't even born on their first wedding. The funny thing is that it's the same Pastor they had for their first wedding. I heard my dad call up his best man from his first wedding as well. It's almost as if these two are truly meant to be. Who would of thought that? Same church. Same pastor. Same Groom.

Weddings kind of give me the creeps because

knowing that this is the last person you're supposed to be with in life is quite scary. Here comes my Dad walking slowly down the aisle to meet my Mom again. He's all crying like a baby. I can't believe the dude is crying. That better be tears of joy, not tears of 'I can't be with Ms. Hamburger anymore.'

"Mr. Rodney L. Lewis, do you take this woman to be your wife, to have and to hold, to love and support through sickness and in health, till death do you part?"

"I do," My father professed.

"And Miss Sandra E. Lewis, do you take Rodney to be your husband, to have and to hold, to love and support through sickness and in health, till death do its part?"

"I do," My mother said with joy.

"By this great State of Florida, by the laws invested in me I now through the hope, trust, and covenant set forth by God for you two, pronounce you husband and wife again. You are now once more Mrs. Sandra E. Lewis. And of course you may now kiss the bride Mr. Rodney L. Lewis."

"Yeah, yeah, Daddy and mommy are one again. Daddy and mommy are one!" Precious shouted out with glee.

I AM THE SECRET!

"I am the work that takes place in many lives. I love those that hate Me and keep watch over those who keep my command. Many people see Me and swear they can't. If only they decide to operate in the measure of faith I've given, they'd see me working all the time.

Most individuals expect Me to come down with a rod of lighting in which I do on some occasions, and others expect to see Me as a giant like the angels back in the day. Perhaps the reason why some see me and some don't, would have to correspond to the urgency of their faith and not My face. Salvation through My Son plays a huge role in how one would let Me help to shape and mold their lives, to be holy.

Most people know me as God while some have heard of me as Alpha and Omega, Prince of Peace, Elohim, El-Shaddai, God almighty, El-Olam the everlasting God. All of that is good, great, and in My perfect will, but at the end of the day, it all means the same. I'm just God. Why do I say that? Because everyday I want my children to feel free to come to me as they would a friend. I'm sure you don't call your neighbor ten different names, then actually ask them a question. No, you don't. So, therefore you don't have to approach me like that. And believe me, your neighbor probably already knows what you want before you ask them. In my case I already knew the questions before you were born. You don't have to use many names, but you do have to come through My Son Jesus.

Am I a jealous God? Yes. Am I a just God? Yes. Am I a loving God? Yes. Just read your Bible and pay particular attention to Exodus chapter twenty.

I, the Great I Am, have done some wonderful things these past ten years in the Lewis family lives. Because I give each one of you free will, I allowed Rodney to cheat, Sandra to get mad at Me and Justin to hate Me. Little Precious, so beautiful and so pure, has stayed innocent and sweet in My sight. I hear every day people asking: how can a great God allow this to happen? Why did it happen to our family?

My simple answer to that question is the very fact that it happened to My son. He was persecuted, beaten, lied on and betrayed right before my very eyes. I could have sent down one angel and destroyed any man that even thought about laying a hand on My Son. Yes, of course I know your very thoughts too, I didn't destroy you because I am God and I love you.

Just like I allowed Sandra to be betrayed and Rodney to feel guilty, so was the betrayal of My son and the guilt of Judas. I am a loving, gracious and forgiving God. I give each man that has ever walked this earth a chance to come to Me, to love Me, and to follow My commandments.

Man's heart is naturally wicked due to the great fall. Satan and his followers roam this earth like a vulture looking for something dead to eat. He is looking for those who will give in to sin and resist holiness.

Because I am God I can do what I want to do and say what I want to say, but I must warn you My will is perfect. I cannot sin, neither do I have a will to sin. I am a just and righteous Ruler over all things ever created both of the earth and the heavens above the earth.

I Am the Secret! To know Me is to love Me, and to keep My words in your heart at all times. I worked through the Art teacher, the Pastor, the Neighbor, and even Alicia. I can work through anyone if they allow me to move into their heart. Sandra allowed me to work on her heart, something that everyone thought was impossible I made possible, because I love to see husband and wife together. Yes, it took ten years for man, but was not even a day for me.

My child Justin got saved, and is making an approach towards me. How much more happier could I be when the angels were singing in heaven when Justin, little Justin accepted Jesus to be his Lord and Savior. Many are called but few are chosen, Justin is a chosen man after My own heart and he will do great things in the future. Yes, he will mess up along the way, but I will place him in a position of power and authority.

I Am the Life Creator! I am the Life Changer! I am God! I am the Secret! Nothing happens without me knowing!"

ABOUT THE AUTHOR

Michael D. Beckford is currently working towards building up his craft as a writer and spreading the news and awareness of his works to whomever is receptive in listening. With a couple hundred books sold for "Beautifully Ugly People!" His main goal is to have all of his books read by the masses, as he continue to work the change that God has put in him to bless others.

ACKNOWLEDGE-MENTS:

I definitely would like to give thanks to my mother Denise Beckford for helping me to spread the word about my previous book "Beautifully Ugly People!" down in Miami. Mom you have been such a blessing and I know that you will tell everyone about this book as well.

I must now give thanks to all those whom has always continued to love, support me and help me out. Please don't take it personal if I didn't mention your name, I thank you too.

Thanks once more to God, Mark and Denise Beckford, Dorothy Wright, Suzette Wright, Sharon Wright, Hollis Wright, Latrice Ivey Robinson, Gary, Mary Elizabeth Edwards Thillips, Rhadi and Tracey Ferguson, Antron Wright, Greg Beckford, Jaunita Beckford, Deon Beckford, Cathie and Victor Beckford, Aunt Helen, Uncle Chip, Uncle Pokey, Uncle Jerome, My brother Matthew, my sisters Latoya and Cherokee. I really appreciate Gary and Ricky Huizenga, Mitchell Clark, the Black Nova Collective, Ms. Deborah Hollis, Mr. and Mrs. Hollis, Ms.

MICHAEL D BECKFORD

Mathe' Harris, Sherica Brown, The Hughes family, Stephen Scavella, Mr. and Mrs. Colbert, Mr. Harvey, Ruth, Dawn Bruce, *Uncle Reece*, Royce and Hannah Lovett, George Britton, Shawanna Henderson, Mr and Mrs. Henderson, Pastor Cyrus Flannigan, Pastor Michael D. Smith, Pastor Susan, Dr. Tellers, Erica Leggett, Jadanis and Krystal Avilus, Marcus and Helena Flournah, Oraine, The LifeGroup, Ms. Seabrook, Larry Hyler, Chakita Hargrove, Napoleon Hinson, Sonship Christian Fellowship, Tremayne Moore, Marilyn Griffith and all of the customers homes I have knocked on the doors of.

I thank you all and may God smile upon each and everyone of you, those whom are mentioned and those whom have not been. As my dad always has said, charge it to my head, not to my heart.

OTHER BOOK TITLES YOU MAY ENJOY BY MICHAEL D. BECKFORD

The Good Christian
The Bad Christian
The Christian
The Perfect Christian
FATHERHOOD
Mila's Big Day! (A Children's Book)

SPECIAL THANKS

To Shantae Charles for once again doing an excellent job in editing this book. Although you were going through some personal trials, you still gave your all in editing this book. I greatly appreciate you for that. You definitely help to keep me accountable in my writing. You are such a blessing and I just wanted to commend you for all that you do, and acknowledge your husband as well.

Darrell Threeths, you have done an excellent job once more. God has truly blessed you with a gift to illustrate. I pray many blessings over your life and your family my brother, and of course I will be happy to work with you on some future projects.

Tracey Leggett, your patience is a mirror of excellence. For anyone to understand my handwriting is a miracle in itself. I truly appreciate you typing up this book to the best quality I could have asked for. Even with your busy schedule with all that you do, I definitely appreciate you taking the time out for me.

Cheryl Jennings, Wow! There is so much to say with so little space. Since the first time I met you at your home selling ADT Security, I felt such a since of comfort right there at your home, once a stranger now a friend, and my publicist as well. I know that we are going to make history together as God blesses both of our publishing companies. I am just so happy to have met you and I send warm wishes to your husband as well.

Brandon Murry (a.k.a. Somethin) I thank you for being one of the first individuals to review and give me feedback on this book. That meant so much to me and I deeply appreciate you for that sir. You are truly a rising star.

Shaumese Massey, I thank you very much for looking over my book for me at such a short period of time. My editor told me to have a third opinion and I appreciate you putting forth an extra effort in me receiving the material on time. May God bless you and continue to inspire you in your writing.

URBAN CLASSICS COLLECTION

Get an instant $5 off This 10 E-Book and Audiobook URBAN CLASSICS COLLECTION **This 10 Ebook 1 Audio Book and 1 Poetry Album bundle is available Exclusively on Gumroad.com***

For **Only $19.99** with instant discount. Order
URBAN CLASSICS COLLECTION Now.